'Disappointed? Were you hoping to return with a scoop?'

Armand went on derisively, '"Armand Broch to Marry"... What a headline for you. I'm sorry to disappoint you! Or are you disappointed for a more...personal reason?'

Calli's head jerked back. Of all the conceited... 'You're the last man in the world I'd——' she began, and stopped, horrified at what she had said, at what she had *revealed*.

Dear Reader

There's something different about Mills & Boon romances! From now on, in the front pages of all our stories, you'll find a short extract to tempt you to read on, a biography about the author and a letter from the editor, all of which we hope will welcome you to our heart-warming world of romance. What's more, if you've got any comments or suggestions to make about Mills & Boon's stories, drop us a line; we'll be glad to hear from you.

See you next month!

The Editor

Elizabeth Duke was brought up in the foothills of Adelaide, South Australia, but has lived in Melbourne ever since her marriage to husband John. She trained as a librarian and has worked in various libraries over the years. These days she only works one day a week, as a medical librarian, which gives her time to do what she loves doing most—writing. She also enjoys researching her books and travelling with her husband in Australia and overseas. Their two grown-up children are now married.

Recent titles by the same author:

WILD TEMPTATION

WHISPERING VINES

BY

ELIZABETH DUKE

MILLS & BOON LIMITED
ETON HOUSE   18-24 PARADISE ROAD
RICHMOND   SURREY   TW9 1SR

*First published in Great Britain 1992
by Mills & Boon Limited*

© Elizabeth Duke 1992

*Australian copyright 1992
Philippine copyright 1992
This edition 1992*

ISBN 0 263 77543 7

*Set in Times Roman 10 on 12 pt.
01-9205-54903 C*

Made and printed in Great Britain

CHAPTER ONE

'I COULD kill him for what he's done to you.' Calli looked at her sister's tear-ravaged face and red swollen eyes and felt a bitter rage swelling inside her. 'The man's a monster! How could he do that to you, Steph—and in the middle of filming, too?'

Only hours earlier Stephanie had been filming on location at Château Broch Winery in the Barossa Valley, South Australia's premier wine-producing district. Her first starring role! And because of what Armand Broch had done to her she had turned her back on her big chance to make a name for herself, fleeing Château Broch before filming was finished, too emotionally traumatised to stay another day, another *hour*. It just showed how deeply Armand Broch had hurt her. Well, you only had to look at her, Calli fumed, to see how much. The man deserved to be whipped!

'They'll replace me, I know they will!' Stephanie sobbed. 'I'll be ruined! Nobody in the industry will ever trust me again. But, Calli, I couldn't stay, I just couldn't! Not after the way he——' She broke down again in a flood of tears.

'Oh, Steph, they won't replace you,' Calli soothed, hiding her own doubts. She knew nothing about the film industry, so how would she know how a director might react? 'Look, as soon as you feel better you can ring them. I'm sure you'll be able to work something out. And then you can go back...'

'I'll never go back—never!' Stephanie shuddered at the thought. 'I couldn't bear to face Armand again. Not after what he did to me. And as for—as for that little slut I caught him with...to have to see her smirking face every day...' She buried her face in her hands. 'I j-just couldn't!'

'They *both* should be whipped,' Calli muttered. 'Do please try to calm down, Steph. They're not worth it.'

'*She* certainly isn't,' her sister agreed, adding peevishly, 'Why do you think she's always chosen to play the "other woman"? The role comes naturally to Roxy Manning, the bitch. But Armand...' She gulped. 'I—I thought he was different. Now I know he was only pretending to love me...only pretending he wanted to marry me...he never meant a word of it! I n-never should have got involved with him! But, Calli, he's so—so damned attractive! I've never met a man with such *charisma*. He's the sexiest man alive...I would have m-married him tomorrow!'

Calli blinked, momentarily diverted. 'You would?' Stephanie had always vowed that marriage was not for her—it would stifle her career; it would stifle *her*. She wanted to be a big star...she wanted to go to Hollywood. And you couldn't do that with a husband dragging on your coat tails.

Stephanie raised a tear-stained face. 'Armand Broch is no ordinary man, Calli. He's head and shoulders above any other man I've ever met. He's Rhett Butler and Heathcliff and Mr Rochester all rolled into one. All man...' Her voice broke on a sob. 'I—I love him, Calli. And I thought he loved me. He's b-broken my heart!' She slumped in her chair, deep sobs racking her slender body.

'Steph, you must try to get some sleep.' Calli frowned worriedly. Stephanie had burst in on her in the middle of breakfast, having arrived on the earliest plane from Adelaide. She'd obviously been up all night. 'While you're resting let me ring your director and explain——'

'No!' Stephanie's head snapped back. 'Nobody's to know what—what really happened. I couldn't bear it. I'd die of shame! You're not to breathe a word, Calli. Promise!' She gripped Calli's arm. 'I never should have come to you!' Tears choked her voice.

Calli patted her arm soothingly. 'Of course you should have come to me, Steph. What are sisters for?' She and her sister—they were *half*-sisters, actually—didn't see each other often. Because of circumstances, and differing interests, they had never been particularly close. But in times of crisis, especially in recent years, Stephanie had tended to turn to Calli for comfort. And Calli was always there for her, ready to help pick up the pieces and patch her flighty sister together again.

'I won't tell a soul, Steph, I promise. Look, I know it must seem like the end of the world to you right now, but once you've had a good sleep I'm sure you'll feel better and be able to work something out with your director. What exactly *did* you tell him before you left?'

'Nothing! I was too upset to speak to anybody. I just left a note saying that I'd been taken ill and needed to go home. What must they be thinking? That I'm on drugs or something! That I've had a breakdown—anything! One thing's for sure,' she said bitterly, 'they're not going to hang around waiting for me. They're on a strict schedule, Calli. Time means money in this business. They'll ditch me and get someone else—I know they will!'

'Oh, Steph, they won't do that.' Calli thought quickly. 'Didn't you say there were only two or three days of filming left to shoot at Château Broch? They're not going to scrap all the work you've done already—not for the sake of a couple of days!'

Stephanie heaved a shuddering sigh. 'You don't know this industry, Calli. They're capable of anything.'

Calli tapped her chin, remembering something. 'You said you told them you were going home, Steph. Your home's in Sydney, not here in Melbourne. They'll try to contact you there if they want to get in touch. Is there someone there I can call? Tell them where you are?'

Stephanie's hand shot out again, her fingers digging into the soft flesh of Calli's arm. 'I don't want anyone to know where I am!' she shrilled. 'That's why I came *here*! I—I'm too upset to speak to anybody yet. Can't you *see* that I'm in no condition——?'

'OK, OK, calm down—I won't tell anyone. Now, Steph, *please*, do try to get some rest. Things will look different after you've had some sleep.' Stephanie had a habit of bouncing back. But would she bounce back this time? Calli wondered anxiously. It was a sign of just how bad a state she was in that she didn't even want to speak to her director. Stephanie's private life was often in a mess, but she had always been thoroughly professional where her acting career was concerned. She had never let anything affect that before.

'I'll never get over this, Calli—never!' Stephanie wailed. 'I feel as if my whole world is crumbling down around me. Armand...my career...and—and as if that's not all...'

'There's *more*?' Calli's heart sank. How much more could her sister take?

Stephanie's eyes—normally so dark and lovely, but now red-rimmed and puffy—brimmed over with tears. 'I—I've lost the diamond out of the ring Mother gave me when she...when she married your father, Calli.'

Stephanie always referred to her stepfather—Calli's father—as 'your' father. She and her stepfather had never got on. Calli's solid, upright father had never been able to come to terms with Stephanie's tempestuous nature, her rebellions, her mood-swings. And at the age of thirteen Stephanie had left their mother's home to go and live with her real father, the charming, erratic ne'er-do-well their mother had divorced years earlier. But that hadn't worked out either, and once again Stephanie had walked out, this time in search of the acting career she had always yearned for and dreamed about. Anything might have happened to her, but somehow, miraculously, she had won a small role in a TV soap. And, give or take a few stops and starts since, she had never looked back.

'You've lost your *diamond*?' Calli shook her head despairingly. Her sister never did things by halves!

'It—it must have popped out last night when——' Stephanie's voice trembled '—when Armand and I were down in his private cellar. He must have knocked it out when he—when he kissed me,' she said with a catch in her voice. 'He had some work to do right after that, so I—so I went to bed...not noticing I'd lost it. Only I—I couldn't sleep. I wanted him so badly! Finally I—I went to his room...and that's when I found him in bed with...that slut!'

Calli asked hastily, 'So you didn't have a chance to go back down into the cellar to look for it? Steph, can't I call——?'

'No!' Stephanie shook her head violently, her mass of black hair tumbling over her beautiful, ravaged face. 'You keep right out of it, Calli! They—they don't know anything about you. They don't even know I *have* a sister! And that's the way I want to keep it. You're my refuge, Calli—someone I can come to when I need to get away from the world. Where nobody can find me. I've lost the diamond, and that's that. I've lost everything now... everything I ever wanted!'

She dissolved into tears again, and it was some time before Calli could calm her down sufficiently to bundle her off to bed.

Calli spent the rest of the weekend worrying about her sister, feeling helpless. She had never seen Stephanie in such a pitiful state before. Her sister had always been dramatic and highly strung—always either on a high or plunged into the depths—but she had never been this bad before. This time she was genuinely suffering, genuinely in despair. It was hard to tell if it was the loss of her lover or the possible loss of her starring role that was affecting her the most. Obviously, it was a combination of both, and the disappearance of her diamond had only compounded her sense of loss. No wonder she thought her whole world was crumbling around her. And whose fault was it? Armand Broch's!

Calli had never been a vengeful person—she had never really hated anybody, certainly not enough to want to extract vengeance. But she vowed in that moment that, if she could ever find a way to get back at Armand Broch for what he had done to her sister, she would seize the chance with both hands. And enjoy every vengeful minute!

*   *   *

'You want me to do a feature on *who*?' Calli stared aghast at her boss Howie Chandler, chief editor of the *Melbourne Star*.

'*Whom,*' Howie corrected, his lips tilting into a grin. 'On Armand Broch. Of Château Broch Wines. Go on, Calli, you must have heard of him. He's rich, he's good-looking, he's single—and he smoulders, as any woman will tell you, with sex appeal. Powerful too. He has a finger in numerous pies other than his winery—restaurants, racehorses, real estate, and goodness knows what else...he works and plays *hard*. And to date no woman has been able to snare the guy. Which makes him one of the most eligible bachelors in the country. And you, my dear Calli, are the lucky one who's been chosen to do a feature on him.'

Calli felt faint. No, she thought. I couldn't. I won't! Not Armand Broch! Even though nearly two months had passed since that terrible Saturday when her sister had come to her in a flood of hysterical tears, Calli's bitter antipathy towards the man who had hurt and humiliated her sister had not diminished, even though her sister's acting career appeared to have been salvaged. No thanks to Armand Broch! After hiding herself away for three miserable days and nights Stephanie had finally managed to pull herself together sufficiently to fly back to Sydney and throw herself on the mercy of her director as he'd arrived back from South Australia. And it was a relieved Stephanie who had called Calli the next day with the good news that she was going to be able to shoot her final scenes in the Sydney studios.

But her sister had still sounded subdued, Calli noted worriedly—a sure sign that her hurt and heartbreak had gone deep. She must still be feeling apprehensive, Calli suspected, about finding future roles. If word got around that Stephanie Fox had walked out while filming was still in progress—for whatever reason—future directors might be wary of taking her on. And that, Calli thought, simply wouldn't be fair!

Howie was eyeing her sideways. 'What's up, Calli? Worried that you won't be up to it?'

Calli seized on the excuse. 'I know nothing about the wine industry...there must be others more——'

'You don't need to know anything about the wine industry. It's the *man* our public is interested in. This is a big scoop for you, Calli. And it's all been arranged.'

'What do you mean—arranged? By who—*whom*?'

'By the big boss...Rex Walters himself!' Howie's crinkled grey eyes were bright with triumph.

Calli's jaw dropped. Rex Walters...international media mogul, and owner of the *Melbourne Star*! He spent most of his time abroad these days, and his rare forays into the *Melbourne Star* office were treated almost like royal visits.

'B-but,' she stammered, 'Mr Walters never interferes in the day to day——'

'Well, he did this time. I prefer to call it using his influence to get a scoop for us. He was most impressed by that feature article you did recently for our weekend magazine, Calli..."A week in the life of Victor Morton". You made an ordinary week in the life of a busy property tycoon into something *extraordinary*, and packed with interest. And your photographs were superb. Mr Walters thinks you're on a winner. He wants you to follow it up with "A week in the life of Armand Broch".'

A *week*! Never! Calli thought, horrified. She wouldn't spend an *hour* in that man's company! 'He—he'd never agree to it,' she blustered, casting around for a way out. 'If he works and plays as hard as you say he does he's not likely to want a journalist with a camera dogging his footsteps for a whole week! I mean . . . wouldn't it cramp his style?'

A slow grin stretched across Howie's weathered face. 'But he's already agreed, my dear Calli. Mr Walters himself has arranged it. I told you.'

Calli bit her lip. If she told Howie how she felt about Armand Broch, and why, he wouldn't be so keen for her to do it! He would see her as being professionally biased—which might colour her article . . .

And it would serve Armand Broch right if it did, she thought, her grey eyes glinting.

But how could she explain to Howie how she felt about Armand Broch without bringing Stephanie into it; without telling him that Stephanie Fox was her half-sister? And that was something she had always kept quiet about here at the newspaper office. She had always been a very private person; she loathed any kind of personal notoriety or publicity, and if Howie or anyone else here at the newspaper knew that the up-and-coming actress was Calli's half-sister they would clamour to know the inside story of their lives together, and they wouldn't be above printing it. They might even try to make some kind of celebrity out of *her*. And she would hate that!

'I wouldn't have thought Armand Broch would be in need of any publicity,' she said in desperation, still grasping at straws.

'You'd be surprised, Calli. There's some lively competition in the Australian wine industry. But apart from that there's a lot of public interest just now in the Château Broch Winery because of this coming movie . . . you know, the one they recently filmed on location there. *The Winemaker*.'

Calli's heart gave a jump. 'Oh, yes?' Her eyes were all innocence as she looked at him.

'People are curious about the winery—and about Armand Broch in particular. It's the right time to do an article, Calli. Broch obviously agrees.'

'When would you want me to do it?' Calli asked in a muffled voice. She felt as if a net were tightening around her.

'Next week. Broch has rearranged his schedule so that he won't have any overseas or interstate trips during the week. Just the odd meeting and appointment in Adelaide, maybe a visit to his stables, that sort of thing. He doesn't like being too far away from his winery at vintage time.'

Calli swallowed. Next week!

'You're not exactly turning handstands.' Howie rolled his eyes in despair. 'I thought you'd be ecstatic.'

Calli tried to pull herself together. 'Does he know who's going to be doing the feature?' she asked helplessly. 'I mean—he might think I'm not well-known enough...'

'Mr Walters showed him the article you did on Victor Morton, and Broch thought it was excellent. Light-hearted without being frivolous. Informative without being too intrusive. In fact, he only agreed to the feature after he was assured that Caroline Barr Smith would be doing it.'

Calli shrugged her shoulders helplessly, knowing that further argument was futile. Caroline Barr Smith was the name she used professionally, to distance herself from plain Calli Smith and to give herself a measure of privacy—Barr being her mother's maiden name, and Caroline her real name, the name on her birth certificate, a name she never used other than professionally. She had been called Calli for as long as she could remember.

'I'd like Armand Broch to know me as Caroline Barr Smith,' she decided on an impulse. She didn't want the hated Armand Broch calling her Calli, like her friends. Besides, it would give her a feeling of security, of anonymity, being known only by her professional name. If Stephanie had mentioned her at all she would have referred to her as Calli, or as Calli Smith. But she hadn't— she had said so. Armand Broch would have no idea that she and Stephanie knew each other, let alone that they were half-sisters.

Which was just as well. After the shabby way he had treated Stephanie he would hardly relish the idea of Stephanie's sister doing a write-up on him. He wouldn't want her anywhere near him!

Calli's eyes narrowed speculatively. No... you wouldn't, would you, Armand Broch? Because I just might expose you for the low-down, two-timing bastard you are, mightn't I? And that wouldn't do your precious image any good at all!

Well, my heartless friend, I can promise you this: if I can find a way to expose you without bringing Stephanie into it—and without jeopardising my professional integrity—I'll damned well do it! What better way to avenge my sister?

After all—her gaze slid purposefully to the pen in her hand—the pen *is* supposed to be mightier than the sword!

She steered her sporty red Mazda through the impressive gates of Château Broch Winery, surprised that she had found the place so easily. Never having been to the Barossa Valley before, she had expected to take a few wrong turns along the way, but her map had been easier to follow than she had expected. She had even arrived earlier than planned.

'A little piece of Germany in typical Australian countryside' was how the valley had been described in her guidebook. Château-like buildings, German sausages, brass bands, and a simply delicious crumble-top cake called *streusalkuchen* mingling happily with the typically Australian native gums, the wattle trees, the iron sheds and the red-gum shingles. A place of rolling hills and gentle sunshine...

A place Stephanie might at one time have called 'home'.

It would never be 'home' to her now.

Knowing that she had time on her hands, Calli brought her car to a smooth halt just inside the gates, where a riot of colour caught her gaze. Rose bushes—hundreds of them—lined the long gravel drive. Was it just co-incidence that there were so many roses here? She re-called that the valley had been named after a winegrowing district in Spain. Barossa...valley of roses. She wound down her window to inhale their sweet fragrance, letting her gaze flicker round.

Shimmering over the slopes in waves of green stretched a sea of vines, the trellises groaning under the weight of the ripe fruit. She could see pickers in brightly coloured shirts and shady hats, and beyond the vines a peaceful lagoon, the water a gleam of blue in the early-afternoon sunlight. Clumps of olive trees, shady eucalypts and towering Norfolk Island pine trees partially masked the iron rooftops and ivy-hung stone walls of the winery buildings. Above a backdrop of dimpled purple hills the sky was a clear, unbroken blue.

A tranquil, beautiful place. No wonder it had been chosen as the site for a film. And no wonder her sister had loved it here. Or was it just the man, the owner, she had loved?

Armand Broch.

The man who had pretended to love her. The man who had led her to believe he wanted to marry her. Until he had callously betrayed her by taking another woman into his bed, breaking poor Stephanie's heart and driving her into hysterical flight, not caring if he wrecked her career at the same time.

Tightening her lips, Calli let the car roll forward, squinting against the dazzling South Australian sun. Beyond the winery buildings she could just make out the pale sandstone walls and small-paned windows of the château itself, an imposing building even from here. Château Broch...the winery's administrative centre—and the home of Armand Broch, the man she was here to write about, to photograph, to follow around like a shadow for a whole week. Well, Armand Broch, if you think I'm going to produce a glowing, fawning little piece you're very much mistaken!

She felt a twinge of guilt at the thought. Until she pictured Stephanie's face, ravaged with grief and shock, and hardened her heart. I'll make him squirm, Steph, don't you worry!

She sighed, marvelling at the irony of fate—or co-incidence—which had brought her here to Armand Broch's doorstep. The man she despised most in all the world—and she would have to kowtow to him, be civil to him, for the next seven days and nights, never showing how she really felt about him! However was she going to manage it?

By being thoroughly professional, that was how!

Coming to the end of the long driveway, Calli pulled into a parking bay, where a number of cars gleamed in

the early-afternoon sun. There was a sign: 'Visitors only.
No cars beyond this point.' Was she a visitor? Not
really—she was here to work, not to buy wine. Unsure
where she ought to go, she clambered out, locked the
car, leaving her camera and luggage safely locked inside,
and headed in the direction of the château to find out.
There was plenty of time before she was due to meet
Armand Broch. Time to get settled in and changed first.

The circular driveway in front of the château was bordered by tall young poplars, their heads bent in the faint
breeze, slender and graceful as peacock feathers. And
there were more roses, their scent mingling with the
heavier, sweeter scent of the vines.

The château itself was as elegantly impressive as any
fine château of Europe. Calli let her gaze run over the
steep roofline, with its spires and turrets, along the pale
yellow sandstone walls and the rows of small-paned
windows with their open green shutters, and thought
poignantly of the heartbreak her sister had suffered
within those thick walls.

'Are you looking for someone?'

She felt a sudden chill as a shadow fell over her, effectively blotting out the sun. She had seen no one, heard
no footsteps approaching. As she swung round she felt
her throat constrict. There was something about the man
who stood there—she thought at once of the word
charisma, Stephanie's word—that told her she was face
to face with Armand Broch himself. Did the impression
come from the man's physical bearing, which was impressive—and very masculine? Or did it come from
within the man himself? There was an unnerving stillness
about him, a watchfulness, that made Calli's skin prickle.

His features were shadowed, the sun striking his dark
hair from behind, illuminating fine chestnut strands that

lifted and fell with the breeze. There was arrogance in
the tilt of his head, strength in the line of his jaw, virility
in every line of his well-proportioned body. He was
wearing black leather trousers and an open-necked white
shirt which showed a disturbing glimpse of tanned flesh.
His hands were firmly planted on his hips, and the sleeves
of his shirt were rolled up, revealing bronzed muscular
arms.

Her senses were instantly on guard, instantly alert,
warning her that here was a man possessed of powerful
inner forces—not least of which were an iron will, a steely
strength, and an awesome self-confidence.

'Well?' His lips moved. 'At a glance, I'd say you're
here after a job, not to buy wine...' She felt his gaze
slide down her slim body, making her uncomfortably
aware of her casual cotton shirt and faded jeans, which
she had intended changing before meeting him. His bold
appraisal was making her feel ill-at-ease in another way
too, making her wonder if it was her clothing he was
scrutinising—or her feminine curves!

She found her voice. She wasn't going to let this man
intimidate her; this man who had been so close to her
sister...until he had cruelly shattered the dreams they
had shared together. The dreams Stephanie had foolishly believed in!

'I am here to work, yes, but——'

'Let me see your hands.'

'I—I beg your pardon?' Puzzled, she held them up.

He took them in his own, running his long fingers
along the smooth white palms, sending a shivery sensation up and down her arms. Repulsion, her logical
mind explained it away, though her nerve-ends seemed
to be calling it something else. Then he turned them over,

and just as lightly traced the fine veins that radiated across their slender white backs.

'How soft and smooth they are...not a blemish. Hardly a worker's hands,' he commented drily.

Her eyes flew to his face, a frown puckering her brow. A *worker's* hands? Surely he didn't think——?

She tried to withdraw her hands then, only to feel his fingers tighten their grip. She let her own grow still, trying not to think about what his touch was doing to her, trying to think instead what it had done to Stephanie.

He raised his head, his eyes seeking hers. She realised she was squinting; the sun was shining directly into her eyes, placing her at a disadvantage. She glanced quickly away, letting her gaze skim over the rows of vines, pretending an interest in the pickers moving among the vines. Anything to avoid the man's discomforting scrutiny!

He was still holding her hands, she realised. It weakened her, and yet at the same time gave her the strength to resist him. This man knew his power over women...and plainly he played on that power. Even Stephanie, who, Calli was well aware, exerted a pretty powerful attraction of her own, had not been proof against it. Had Armand Broch ever really loved her sister? Or had he been playing some kind of cruel game with her—the way he was now playing with *her*, Stephanie's sister?

CHAPTER TWO

CALLI found the strength to pull her hands away at last, abruptly clenching them into fists to stop their shaking. She was finding it difficult to speak. The prospect of introducing herself as Caroline Barr Smith had caused her throat to dry up. She considered forgetting about her little subterfuge and telling Armand the truth—that she was plain Calli Smith, Stephanie Fox's sister. But she knew she would be out on her ear if she did, and Howie would be furious with her for not telling him the truth before she took on the assignment. And she would have lost her chance to expose Armand Broch—assuming she could have found a subtle way to do it without making it into a personal attack.

Before she answered she managed to shift neatly sideways, so that now it was he who faced into the sun.

'Please, let me explain who I——'

That was as far as she got. She saw his hand come up; gave a slight gasp as he cupped her chin in his strong lean fingers, forcing her to turn and look up at him. She caught her breath as she met his eyes—eyes as green as the vines, ringed by tiny splinters of gold. In the sunlight they glittered like fiery emeralds.

She felt his magnetism like a physical shock. A voice whispered a warning. Stephanie had felt that same magnetism... and now she was suffering for it.

To avoid those startling eyes she fastened her gaze on the deep cleft in his chin. She wanted to shake off his hand, but didn't dare. If she hoped to keep her assignment she had better not alienate him from the start.

'What do you think our harsh Barossa Valley sun will do to that delicate complexion of yours?' he drawled.

Calli felt a faint smile tugging at her lips, headily aware that for the moment *she* had the advantage over Armand Broch.

'I won't be *working* in the sun—as far as I'm aware,' she said blandly. 'Though if I had to I could always borrow a hat.'

He slackened his grip on her chin, though she remained burningly aware of his fingers still resting there. 'What do you mean—you won't be working in the sun?' he demanded. 'All our pickers work out in the sun.'

'I'm the journalist from the *Melbourne Star*,' she said sweetly. A trifle breathlessly.

His hand, mercifully, dropped away at last, though it left her skin still tingling from his touch.

'*You're* . . .' She saw comprehension dawning in the green depths. 'Oh, hell.'

'You *are* Armand Broch, aren't you?' she challenged, trying to keep her antipathy for him out of her voice as she mouthed the despised name.

He nodded, his firm lips lifting in a rueful smile, making the cynical lines etched into his cheeks less noticeable. 'So you're Caroline Barr Smith... Why the hell didn't you say so?'

'You gave me little chance,' she bit back, remembering the way he had cut her off each time she had tried to speak, seizing her hands, grabbing her chin, imposing his will on whom he thought was a defenceless, out-of-work female seeking a job as a grape-picker!

'No wonder you didn't look like the usual prospective picker,' he murmured without apology. 'Though I can't say you look like my idea of a journalist either!' His gaze flicked over her faded jeans and shirt, and came to rest on her flushed face and the lock of smooth honey-blonde hair which had slipped down over one eye. 'Well, Miss Barr——'

'Caroline,' she invited with a lift of her chin. Well, she thought, the die is cast. I'm Caroline now... Calli has ceased to exist, for this week at least.

'Caroline.' A flicker in the green was his only response. 'I was expecting someone a bit... older,' he said musingly, eyeing her in a way that made the fine hairs on the back of her neck lift warily. What did he mean by that? she wondered uneasily. Had he been hoping for someone more sophisticated, more worldly... someone closer to his own age, perhaps—he must be in his mid-thirties at least, while she was barely twenty-three—who would be more likely to play the sort of games he enjoyed playing with women? Someone he could have had a bit of fun with for the week they were together, in the comforting knowledge that his journalist guest, being a hard-boiled woman of the world, wouldn't be likely to take his attentions too seriously?

Well, Armand Broch, she mused, tightening her lips, you have no need to be wary of me, young and suscep-tible though I might look to you. You're the last man on earth I'd ever want to be involved with.

Aloud she said coldly, 'I understood you were fam-iliar with my work, Mr Broch. What has my age got to do with it?'

His lip curled faintly, and she felt a twinge of an-noyance. Her prickly answer seemed to have given him the impression that she was sensitive about her age, her inexperience!

'My staff normally call me Armand,' he told her with a brief lift of his broad shoulders. He was still watching her, she noted edgily, holding his gaze with an effort. 'You might as well too. We're an informal bunch here. Disciplined—but informal.'

She wondered how disciplined he had been on the night Stephanie had caught him in bed with another woman! Had his discipline faltered then? Had he suffered any shame, any remorse at all? No, she brooded, trying to keep her expression bland, to mask the bitterness she felt. Looking at him—at that arrogant, mocking face— he hadn't suffered in any way whatsoever. Stephanie was the only one suffering!

Even knowing the kind of man he was, she had to consciously steel herself against the power of those compelling green eyes. 'Armand,' she forced the despised name out, 'I apologise for not being more...suitably dressed. I planned to change before making myself known to you.'

His lip quirked upward in a way she would have found devastatingly attractive in anyone else but Armand Broch. 'Feel free to dress as you please,' he said indifferently. 'Freshen up and change by all means, if you feel the need.' His gaze flicked away with a faint frown. 'How did you get here? Where is your luggage?'

'I came in my own car. I left it in the visitors' car park.'

'You drove all the way from Melbourne? By yourself?'

'Yes. I thought it might be handy to have my own car——'

'You won't need it,' he said curtly. He seemed faintly irritated. Didn't he *want* her to have any independence in the week she was here? Did he expect her to be with him every minute of every day?

She eyed him speculatively. Surely a man of Armand Broch's appetites where women were concerned would want at least *some* time to himself? No normal man would want a journalist following him around like a shadow on the nocturnal excursions he was notorious for! If he did he must be sicker and more debauched than she'd imagined. And he would deserve whatever she wrote about him!

'You're looking very fierce,' he said, his eyes burning into her own, so that it was an effort to meet them without flinching. 'Anyone would think you were planning a quick getaway!'

He said it jokingly, but there was an odd nuance in his voice that brought her chin up sharply. There was something faintly menacing in his tone... or was she imagining it?

'Do women who come to Château Broch often need to make a quick getaway?' she retorted lightly, without thinking, only to feel her face flame as she thought of Stephanie. Her poor sister had certainly been forced to make a quick getaway... in a desperate need to escape the humiliation and heartbreak that Armand Broch had callously subjected her to. How many other women had he hurt and humiliated in the same way?

She saw Armand's eyes narrow, and there was a silvery glint in them now that frightened her. Was he angry at what she had said? Or had he noticed her flush, and concluded that she might be after *him*?

'Only joking,' she said hastily, backing away slightly. 'Where would you like me to put my car?'

His answer was abrupt. 'Bring it up to the house. I'll get someone to put it in one of our garages.' His disturbing gaze veered away at last, and she breathed a sigh of relief. As she was about to move off he said, 'When you've taken out your luggage I'll get Agnes, our house-keeper, to show you to your room. You can have the guest room that Lauren uses at times.'

'Lauren?' Calli echoed, pausing. Yet another of his women? she wondered nastily, with a tiny prickle of jealousy on Stephanie's behalf.

Armand looked down at her, his face coldly im-passive. 'My private secretary. Lauren lives in Nuriootpa, and normally travels here daily, though occasionally she has acted as my hostess at official functions and formal dinners and has stayed the night.'

Stayed the night...played hostess... What else had Armand Broch's obliging secretary done for him? Calli wondered waspishly, while carefully masking her thoughts.

'Maybe I'll ask you to do the same for me, if an oc-casion should arise this week when I need a hostess,' he murmured, and she bit back a gasp of horror. It was bad enough having to write about the man, but to act as his hostess...that was asking too much!

Their gazes locked for a moment—his green eyes probing and faintly mocking, her grey ones revealing in that fleeting instant her antipathy for the man.

'The idea doesn't appeal to you?' he challenged, and she wasn't sure if it was surprise or irritation she saw in his eyes. Surprise, most likely, she thought wryly. He'd expect any woman to jump at the opportunity, the ego-tistical rake!

'You think that acting as hostess would come outside your working brief?' he drawled. 'Or...could it be that you're worried you might make a hash of it?'

Her eyes snapped, throwing out silver sparks. 'If I seem reluctant it's because I wouldn't want people getting any wrong ideas...I wouldn't want them to think...'

She hesitated, biting her lip. To think what she had immediately thought about Lauren?

'You wouldn't want them thinking that you're just another of Armand Broch's women?' he spelt out baldly, his eyes glinting.

She flushed. 'So you admit you're a womaniser,' she shot back without thinking.

At once the green eyes turned to ice. 'Ah...so you have preconceived ideas about me, have you, Caroline Barr Smith?'

She tried to retrieve the situation. 'You said yourself——' she began, but he cut her off with an impatient,

'I'm aware that I have a certain...reputation where women are concerned. Men in my position are always a target for gossip and innuendo. Not that I'm saying I live like a monk—far from it. But so what? I'm a free man, Caroline...I'm not hurting anybody.'

No? she thought bitterly, letting her thick lashes sweep down to hide the flare of rancour in her eyes. Only the women you have cast aside after you've tired of them and want to take up with someone else! Only the women you've fooled into believing you love and want to marry, so that you can get what you want from them...never meaning a single word!

His eyes narrowed. 'Write about me as you find me, Caroline, not as others see me.' She would have sworn there was a faint threat in his tone. *As she found him...* Did he intend to be on his best behaviour all week, then, so that she would write nothing but good about him?

'I consider myself a professional, Mr Broch,' she said coolly. 'And I assure you that what I write in my article, and what I show through my photographs, will be the truth...as *I* see it.'

She realised at the same time that she must be more careful in future to hide her feelings. She didn't want him guessing that she had been speaking to Stephanie. That might lead to the truth coming out that she was Stephanie's sister. And he would never agree to let her write about him if he knew that. Not after what he had done to her sister. And if that happened she would never have the opportunity to expose him for what he really was.

'I'll go and get my car,' she said, swinging away, wanting to hide the surge of bitterness she felt rising inside her, bitterness for this man who had been so callously indifferent to the woman who had loved him and believed in his lies. Didn't he have an ounce of feeling for Stephanie, for the suffering he had caused her?

As she brought her car to a halt at the foot of the ballustraded steps leading up to the front door of the château Armand was waiting for her with an older man wearing a cap and overalls.

'Ben Yates...Caroline Barr Smith,' Armand said briefly. 'Ben will put your car away, Caroline, after you've taken out whatever you'll need.'

'I've just one case and my camera,' Calli said, opening the boot. 'I can manage,' she said as Armand stepped forward to help her with her suitcase. He took no notice, taking the case from her, leaving her to carry the camera.

A graceful fountain played near the front steps. The tinkle of cascading water had a soothing effect on Calli as she followed Armand up the wide steps to a heavily panelled double door. Voluminous shrubs and attractive ornamental trees on either side of the steps screened the lower-floor windows.

At Armand's ring a middle-aged woman in a neatly pressed grey dress appeared. Close-set brown eyes looked Calli up and down, making her wish she'd never worn her faded blue jeans.

'Caroline, I'd like you to meet Agnes. Agnes— Caroline Barr Smith, the journalist from the *Melbourne Star*,' Armand explained as the woman's eyebrows rose fractionally. He ushered Calli into the château's palatial cream and gilt entrance hall. A murmur of delight dropped from Calli's lips as she took in the delicate baroque furnishings, the marble busts and the elegant crystal chandeliers. A sweeping staircase dominated one end of the spacious hall.

'Agnes will take you to your room, Caroline. When you have unpacked and changed——' Armand's eyes swept over her as he handed her her suitcase '—come to my office. Unless you are tired and want to rest?' His brow shot up.

'No...I'm fine.' She did feel a bit weary after her long drive, but she hated sleeping in the middle of the day. She would rather have an early night and sleep the night through.

'Agnes will show you where my office is. Agnes, how about preparing some tea while Caroline is unpacking? I'll be up as soon as I've had a word with Leila.'

Who was Leila? Calli wondered as he vanished through a pair of hand-carved antique walnut doors, his footsteps echoing starkly on the polished redwood parquetry floor.

'The bedrooms are upstairs,' Agnes muttered, leading the way.

'It's a lovely place,' Calli ventured. She was anxious to win the housekeeper's approval. Live-in staff were generally mines of information—if they could be persuaded to talk.

The woman sniffed, as if she thought of the place only in terms of the amount of work it meant to her. Or was it that she simply didn't like journalists? Especially *probing* journalists, who were planning to stay for a whole week, digging into people's private lives and at the same time making extra work for her?

'Part of the château is living quarters, the rest is office accommodation,' Agnes volunteered with a shrug. 'There are private cellars underneath.' Ah, yes, Calli remembered. Armand Broch's private cellar...where Stephanie had lost her diamond. She must look for it while she was here. That diamond had meant a lot to her sister.

'The winery and tasting-rooms are in separate buildings. I suppose someone will show you round some time. So you're here to write about Mr Broch...?' The small dark eyes slid round to rest on Calli's face in frank curiosity. And some mistrust, Calli suspected.

'People are interested in Mr Broch—and in his winery,' she said, nodding. 'Especially with that movie being filmed here.' She looked enquiringly at the housekeeper, hoping Agnes would take it from there. But her only comment was a grunt.

'I suppose it made a lot of extra work for you.' Calli was sympathetic. 'Did they all stay here at the château?'

'Hardly. Only the stars and the director. The rest of the crew brought caravans and lived in those.'

As they reached the top of the stairs Calli drew in a careful breath.

'I'm a great fan of Stephanie Fox's. She's a marvellous actress.' She let her breath out in a sigh. 'And so beautiful! I'm surprised Hollywood hasn't snapped her up.'

'She was a good looker all right. As dark as you are fair. When she flashed those black eyes of hers she could get anything she wanted. Or thought she could.'

'What do you mean?' Calli asked innocently. Was Agnes about to open up about Stephanie's abortive love-affair with Armand? What did Agnes think about the shabby way her employer had treated the woman he had made out he loved and wanted to marry? Or was the housekeeper used to the way Armand treated his women, the lies he told them? What, Calli wondered, had happened to Roxy Manning, the woman Armand had thrown Stephanie over for—'that little slut', as her sister had called her, who had played the 'other woman' in the movie? Had she, in turn, since been thrown over?

'I don't mean anything,' Agnes said gruffly. The loyal housekeeper, Calli thought, hiding a sigh. Best not to ask about Roxy Manning just now. That would be pushing her luck a bit far.

She made one last attempt to draw the housekeeper out. 'They say that Miss Fox and Mr Broch...' She paused deliberately, leaving the rest hanging. She didn't want to push it. As a journalist, she knew Agnes would be wary of her, especially to begin with.

There was a short, palpable silence. Then, 'That's all over,' Agnes said abruptly.

Calli assumed surprise. 'Oh, that's a shame...' She gave an airy shrug. 'I—um, I understood they were thinking of getting married.'

The housekeeper looked at her sharply. 'Where did you hear that? That's rubbish!'

Calli mentally rapped her knuckles. Stephanie and Armand must have kept their decision to marry a close secret. Well, Armand would, she thought bitterly—he never had intended to marry her sister! She felt like kicking herself for opening her mouth about it, risking giving herself away. Because, even if Armand *had* told Agnes and other members of his household that he was planning to marry Stephanie, fooling them the same way he had fooled Stephanie, Agnes was unlikely to admit it. Especially not to a journalist. She would want to protect Armand from any bad publicity, being aware now that he had never had any intention of marrying the actress.

You've put your foot in it, Calli Smith, she chided herself as she followed Agnes across the landing at the top of the stairs. You'd better get yourself out of this one quick smart, before Agnes repeats this conversation to Armand, and he wonders how you *knew*.

'I must have read it or heard it somewhere,' she said hastily. 'You know how people gossip when an actress is involved with anybody. People are always speculating about whether they're going to end up getting married. Anyway, you say it's over now... thank you for telling me that. I believe in getting my stories *accurate*,' she assured Agnes righteously. 'You need have no fear that I will be filling my article with gossip and hearsay. I'm not that sort of a journalist.' No, she thought ruefully. What I write in my article will be the absolute truth. No matter how unflattering it might be to Armand Broch!

Agnes gave a grunt, but she seemed satisfied. She led Calli through a long gallery lined with family portraits. Members of the Broch family, Calli assumed. The forbidding faces seemed to be watching her with cold suspicion. As well they might, she mused with a stab of misgiving.

'Are Mr Broch's parents here?' she asked curiously.

'Only Mr Broch senior—he died last year,' Agnes said.

'His mother is still alive?' Calli asked.

Agnes shrugged. 'You ask a lot of questions,' she bristled. 'I thought it was Mr Broch you were supposed to be writing about.'

Calli realised her mistake. She was pressing too hard. If she wasn't careful she would end up alienating Agnes, and then the woman might clam up altogether.

'I always add a little family background,' she explained hastily. 'Never mind, Agnes. I'll ask Mr Broch.'

'You can try,' Agnes said enigmatically, almost pushing Calli into a high-ceilinged room brightened by the slanting rays of the afternoon sun, which cast a pool of dusky gold across the fluffy chartreuse carpet.

Calli was still puzzling over Agnes's remark after the housekeeper left her alone to unpack and freshen up, having first pointed out the bathroom next door. 'I'll be back in twenty minutes to take you to Mr Broch's office,' the woman said as she left.

Alone at last, Calli took a closer look at the room. A fine room for a mere working journalist! Genuine antique furniture. Exquisite pieces of porcelain. Heavy pink brocade silk drapes and a matching bedspread. A splendid carved four-poster bed. A *double* bed, she noted with a faint curl of her lips.

She recalled Armand telling her that it was the room his secretary had used on occasion. How very convenient, she thought sourly, having a double bed in here!

No doubt all Armand Broch's guest rooms—including the one Stephanie had used while she was here— had double beds too! And no doubt Stephanie's room had been conveniently close to *his* room, wherever that was.

Calli's eyes narrowed derisively. What a set-up he has here—the female-devouring Bluebeard!

Well, he's not going to devour *me*, she vowed—only to chuckle ruefully at the very idea that he might want to. Men like Armand Broch didn't waste their time pursuing unworldly little journalists with delicate complexions and outmoded scruples...not when they were used to pursuing more meaty game—tempestuous black-eyed movie stars, for example.

And, anyway, he was hardly likely to try anything, knowing he would be taking the risk of having it publicised over half the country! Which made her pretty safe, thank goodness.

She was frowning as she threw her suitcase on to the bed. *Meaty game*... Her own phrase drifted back. Was that all Stephanie had ever been to Armand Broch—a game, a challenge, someone to hunt down and conquer? Was that how he looked on all women? As fair game...to be hunted, and played with, and, once he had tired of the chase, and tired of *them*, discarded without a second thought?

Well, Armand Broch, she swore, I intend to find out precisely what sort of man you really are, and, you can rest assured, I won't be squeamish about telling the truth in my article. I can promise you that!

CHAPTER THREE

AGNES left Calli at the door of Armand's office. Calli knocked before pushing the door open, only to pause as she heard him say, 'But I *need* you, sweetheart...'

Realising he was on the phone, she started to back out again, but he beckoned her in, still talking into the phone.

'Let's talk about it over dinner... I'll bring a bottle of bubbly. And I can assure you, Davina, my pet... I intend to be *very* persuasive.'

I'll bet you're a past master at that, Calli thought tartly. Was that how you got around Stephanie, you loathsome Lothario? By telling her you *needed* her? Can't you let a single day go by, not even a Sunday, without needing a woman?

As Armand replaced the receiver she wiped all expression from her face.

He ran his eyes approvingly over her cool ice-blue dress, noting how the skirt flared from her slender waist to reveal slim stockinged legs and well-shaped feet in low-heeled sandals, and drawled, 'Mm... that's better.'

Her fair hair, earlier tumbling in a silken mass to her shoulders, was now pulled back into a businesslike knot behind. She had added a dab of powder and lipstick— more to give herself courage than for reasons of vanity. Here, in this proximity to Armand Broch, she needed all the courage she could muster. If he should ask her any personal questions she needed to be able to keep her cool and give satisfactory answers—without giving herself away.

At least there was no fear of Armand seeing any family likeness between herself and Stephanie. Her sister had the dark, dramatic good looks of her father, Dillon Fox, while she, Calli, had the straight fair hair and calm grey eyes of their mother. And, having lived apart for so long, it was unlikely that they would share any common mannerisms or facial expressions that might have given her away. Even their voices were different, Stephanie having long since trained her voice into a throaty, theatrical drawl, with no trace of an Australian accent, while Calli still had the soft, melodic voice she had always had, gently but undeniably Australian.

'Agnes will be back in a minute with some tea.' Armand rose from his desk and came round to pull up a chair for her. 'Why don't you sit down?'

'Thank you.' As she sat down she looked up at him— only to feel again the power of those startling green eyes. She let her gaze slide away, down the cynical line of his cheek to the fine crease which ran from his throat to his hairline, where the dark hair curled softly into the nape of his tanned neck.

'You don't look as if you've been driving all day.' Armand's tone was admiring. 'You look as fresh as a daisy. Charming.'

Instinctively she flinched at the compliment. She could do without compliments from Armand Broch, her sister's callous ex-lover. She tried to hide her distaste, but it was difficult. How many women had he had since he'd thrown Stephanie over for that—for that——?

'You have an intriguingly expressive face, Caroline,' Armand commented. And to her alarm he reached out and touched her cheek with his hand. The touch of his fingertips had the effect of a hot iron scorching her skin. Much as she wanted to jump up and run, much as she wanted to fling his sentiments back in his face, she forced herself to stay put—even managing a tight little smile.

She felt unutterable relief when his hand dropped away. But she noticed that Armand was eyeing her oddly as he took a step back.

'I suppose you're curious about our set-up here,' he said, propping himself on the edge of his desk. But there was a faint coldness in his voice now, as if he was reluctant or resentful at her presence here, and his eyes were hard as they met hers. He looks on me as an interloper, it struck Calli. He doesn't want me here. But, damn it, *I* didn't chase him for this assignment! I had to be talked into it.

'The general office is downstairs, with its own rear access, making it quite separate from the private living areas,' Armand went on. 'The office staff come in six days a week—they all live locally. Lauren, my secretary, spends part of her time down there and part of her time up here, working in the adjoining room...' He waved a hand.

When she's not engaged in extra-curricular activities with her boss, no doubt... Calli eyed him coolly.

'Ah...here's Agnes with our tea.'

Agnes set down a tray on the desk, and as they sipped their tea and nibbled fresh scones Armand asked, 'Are you familiar with wineries at all?' His eyes seemed to pierce hers as he asked the question—as if he expected her to have done some homework on the subject before coming here.

'I've visited one or two.'

'Which ones?' His tone seemed unnecessarily sharp, and she recalled what Howie had said about compe-

tition between the various wineries. Was that what was
behind it?

'I—I can't remember,' she said honestly. 'It was some
time ago——'

'You can't *remember*?' he barked. 'What kind of
journalist are you, for goodness' sake?'

'I—I wasn't on an assignment or anything,' she de-
fended herself, tilting her chin. 'They were just private
visits. A wine-tasting weekend at one of the Rutherglen
wineries in Victoria... and a visit to a winery somewhere in the Hunter Valley, when I was there on holiday
a couple of years ago. This is my first visit to the Barossa
Valley. To any South Australian winery, for that
matter... that I can recall.'

'Are you always as vague as this about the places
you've visited?' he asked irritably.

'I'm not vague about my work,' she was quick to
retort. 'You can rest assured that everything I write about
you and your winery will be well researched and dead
accurate.'

Rather than mollifying him, that seemed to annoy him
too. 'There's no need to go into too much detail. And
if you intend to do any research while you're here I'd
like you to have someone with you while you're doing
it. I don't want you just wandering around on your own.
You understand?'

'Perfectly,' she said levelly, but she was puzzled by his
vehemence. Was he concerned about her safety? Or was
he worried that she might reveal something about his
winemaking process that he wanted to keep secret? Was
competition between the wineries as fierce as that? she
wondered.

'Look, you might as well know,' he said, as if he
realised how he must have sounded, 'I wasn't keen on

this idea...having a journalist trailing around after me for a whole week. I look on it as...an intrusion.'

I'll bet you do, Calli thought nastily, thinking of Stephanie and his other women. She looked up at him. 'Then why did you——?' she began, only to be cut off in mid-sentence.

'Rex Walters twisted my arm. He pointed out the benefits, in terms of publicity...and the fact that there's a lot of interest just now in that movie I stupidly agreed to have filmed here. Even so, I was still tempted to say no, but I owed Rex a favour. He supported me when I was going through a rough patch here a few years ago, after a fire had all but wiped us out...when I needed some public exposure to get back on my feet.'

'I see.' Well, at least she knew now why he wasn't exactly falling all over her like other public figures she had interviewed in her time, who would have done anything for a bit of publicity. Armand had needed to have his arm twisted, only agreeing because he felt indebted to Rex Walters. Armand Broch wouldn't be a man who would care to be indebted to anyone, Calli suspected. He struck her as being very much his own man. 'All man', as Stephanie had once described him.

At the thought of Stephanie her expression hardened.

'Perhaps you would like to see the view from the balcony,' Armand suggested in a somewhat milder tone. 'And then I'll take you over the winery and introduce you around.'

She nodded and rose, following him as he marched over to the long french windows and flung them open. Beyond him she glimpsed a wide stone balcony, bordered by a sculptured stone wall.

As she stepped out on to the shaded balcony a sharp breeze struck her face, curling round her ears in a soulful whine. Involuntarily she shivered.

'Is it too cold out here for you?' Armand's voice came from above her left shoulder, dangerously close. She felt a moment of panic, afraid he was going to place a protective arm around her shoulders. If he did, would she be able to hide her repulsion at his touch?

'Not at all,' she said hastily, and grimaced as she heard the brittleness in her voice. 'It's invigorating.' Moving away from him, she gulped deep breaths of fresh air. 'Mm...the air here is so pure!'

'Feel free to come out here and breathe in the air any time you like,' Armand invited, and there was a dryness, a mocking note in his voice. Had he realised how his nearness had affected her?

In her embarrassment, and her agitation, she was tempted to swing round and shout accusingly at him, 'How could you have hurt my sister the way you did? Don't you realise what you've done to her?' Luckily she managed to restrain herself in time, knowing it would be disastrous if she did. She would be out of here in three seconds flat, with no story—and probably no job!

'Over there is the library...' Armand was pointing across the balcony. 'You're welcome to go in there any time you like.'

He was spelling out the ground rules... the places she could go, the places she couldn't—at least, not unaccompanied.

'Am I permitted to go for a walk among the vines?' she asked with a faint dryness of her own.

'By all means.' The green eyes glinted. 'On a hot day you might even like to take a dip in the lagoon. It's quite safe.'

As long as you're not around at the time, her eyes told him. Then, afraid that he might have read too much in the look, she swung her head away and stared down at the cold flagstones way below. She stifled a sigh as Stephanie's tear-stained face drifted back to haunt her. Armand might just as well have tossed her sister over the balcony on to those flagstones... he could hardly have hurt her any more than he had. As far as Calli knew, Stephanie had never been rejected by a man before, least of all for another woman. Knowing Stephanie, that must have been almost as devastating as losing the man she loved.

'Well? Is the view up to your expectations?'

The fine hairs rose at the nape of her neck as she felt Armand's presence close behind her. There was a scathing note in his voice that sent a faint tremor through her. Had he realised that her mind was far away... that she hadn't even been looking at the view? Would he be wondering *why*?

Without turning her head, she let her eyelids flutter upward. 'It's breathtaking,' she said, summoning all her resources to keep her voice steady—and to inject some enthusiasm. It wasn't too difficult. The view *was* breathtaking. She enthused aloud, 'The view over the valley... the blue hills... the rows and rows of vines...and,' she glanced down, 'the roses in the garden beds below...' Let him think she had been admiring those. They were certainly worthy of admiration, she realised now, running her gaze over the profusion of red and pink and gold blooms. 'I adore roses,' she heard herself babbling on. 'They are my favourite flower. I can smell their scent from here.'

'We'll have to get Agnes to put some in your room,' Armand said, and Calli was relieved to hear the amused tolerance in his voice, erasing for now the cold cynicism that was so often there.

'You must love them too,' she said impulsively. 'You have them everywhere.'

'I do admire them, but there's a practical reason for having them here. Roses actually play a part in vine-yards, acting as an early-warning sign for mildew. My sister Leila is responsible for planting the rose bushes— more than two thousand of them. She used to be a horticulturalist, only she spends most of her time helping out here at the winery these days.'

'She lives here too?' Calli asked. What did his sister think of her brother's sexual exploits? she wondered acidly. Surely she didn't approve!

Armand nodded. 'She married my chief winemaker Hamish a couple of years ago. They both live here, though Leila says they'll move out when she starts a family... or when I decide to marry and settle down, whichever comes first.' His lip curled. 'I strongly doubt that it will be the latter,' he added in a sardonic drawl.

'You never intend to marry?' Calli asked, keeping her tone light with an effort. And I'll bet you never did intend to marry, even at the time you were proposing to Stephanie, even when your treacherous lips were convincing her that you loved her and wanted her for your wife!

'I've never met a woman yet that I'd want to spend the rest of my life with,' he said, cynicism heavy in his voice. 'Let alone to be the mother of my children.'

You...rat, she thought, inwardly fuming. And yet it's OK for you to let a woman *believe* you want to marry her. Obviously Armand Broch was a man who would promise anything to get a woman into his bed and keep her there until he was ready to take up with someone else! One of these days, Calli fumed silently, some woman will slap a breach-of-promise suit on you, Armand Broch—and then you'll be sorry!

'You look a bit put out, Caroline,' Armand said derisively. 'Disappointed? Were you hoping to return with a scoop? "Armand Broch to Marry..." What a headline for you. I'm sorry to disappoint you! Or are you disappointed for a more... personal reason?'

Her head jerked back. Of all the conceited...

'You're the last man in the world I'd——' she began, and stopped, horrified at what she had said, at what she had *revealed*. 'I mean——' She broke off in confusion, blushing scarlet.

'You sound as if you really do mean it,' he murmured with a twist of his lips. 'Well, that's refreshing, at any rate.' He seemed surprised rather than angry. Of course, he would be, she thought balefully. As one of Australia's wealthiest, most eligible bachelors, he must have women chasing after him all the time—and be heartily sick of it. What a relief it must be for him to know that he wasn't going to have that problem with *her*.

'You have other sisters or brothers?' she asked, anxious to change the subject.

'I have a brother, Kurt—Leila's twin brother—who lives in McLaren Vale, south of Adelaide, where we have extensive vineyards—even more extensive than the ones we have here. The grapes are brought here to be processed. All our winemaking activities,' he explained, 'are centralised here in the valley.'

She found herself gulping in some more fresh air while he was talking, the neutral topic helping her to regain her composure. His voice was rich and low-pitched, with an intriguing inflexion that Calli had to admit would cast a spell over almost any woman. Even knowing what a louse he was, she wasn't indifferent to it—or to him. He was a dangerously attractive man. Thank goodness she knew him for what he really was!

'Let's go down now and meet Leila and Hamish...I'm afraid none of us will be at home this evening to have dinner with you.' He didn't sound particularly apologetic! 'Leila and Hamish are going to Kurt's, and I have a dinner in town.'

Yes...I already know, Calli answered silently. You made no secret of it...of how much you *need* your Davina.

'Agnes will bring something up to your room. I guess you'll be wanting to retire early and get a good night's sleep before you start on this damned assignment of yours in the morning.'

'That's...thoughtful of you,' she said with difficulty. Thanking Armand Broch for anything tended to stick in her throat. Or perhaps he wasn't being so thoughtful...perhaps he just wanted her out of the way— or to know where she was—while everyone was out!

He waved her back into his office, and as she stepped past him her bare arm brushed against his, and she was sizzlingly aware of the potent animal magnetism flowing from his warm skin to hers. Appalled at her reaction, she squeezed her hand into a fist to break the spell, and hurried ahead of him into the room.

As they stepped out into the sunshine, having taken the back stairs down through the deserted offices on the ground floor, the sun's dying rays spread a welcome warmth over them after the relative coolness of the château. Somewhere in the trees a kookaburra laughed and another cackled a reply.

'I'll show you where the grapes come in first,' Armand said, leading the way. They spent a few moments in the receival area, talking with Charlie, the assistant wine-maker, a giant of a man who was prowling around, anxiously assessing the quality of the grapes as they were brought in. The air was heavy with the pungent scent of ripe grapes, and Armand looked well-pleased as he asked, 'Where's Hamish?'

'He was here a few minutes ago. He must have gone back to the lab.'

'We'll catch up with him later.' Armand steered Calli into the processing plant, and, after watching the giant grape-crushing plant in action and the pre-drainer separating the juices, they moved on to inspect the shining temperature-controlled fermenting tanks. Everyone they met seemed to be busy doing something, as well they might, since this was vintage time.

Armand introduced her simply as, 'Caroline Barr Smith, from the *Melbourne Star*.'

'Where's your camera?' someone called out at one point.

'I don't actually start work until tomorrow,' she answered with a smile, hoping that the fact that she wasn't on the job yet would help to break the ice. It certainly appeared to be helping. Everyone was being friendly, at least to her face.

The blending cellar and maturing storage-rooms were housed in ivy-hung buildings of handhewn yellow sand-stone, their turrets and arched doorways and small arched windows lending them an old-world charm and character. Armand explained each process in a simple, informative way, and Calli found it all so interesting that she couldn't hold back her questions—and was surprised at how readily he answered them, with none of the wariness she had expected, after the warning he had given her earlier about poking her nose in where she shouldn't. Maybe, after all, he had been thinking of her safety, and as long as she didn't wander around on her own she could see and ask anything.

'You'll notice the change of temperature in here,' he commented as they moved to the maturing cellars. Inside, the sudden chill brought goose-bumps to her arms, and she found herself rubbing them unconsciously.

Casks, both large and small, were stacked in rows, often reaching to the ceiling. In the bottle-maturing cellar every inch of space was utilised, other than the necessary passageways, and in here, where the ceiling-high rows of bottles were like solid walls pressing in on both sides, Calli was acutely conscious of Armand's closeness, of the faint scent of aftershave wafting from his skin, of his virile masculinity, which seemed to emanate from him in waves. She had to swallow hard before she could speak—and when she did her voice sounded strangely hollow and unlike her own.

'There must be hundreds—thousands of bottles in here,' she said. Anything to take her mind off the effect he was having on her! How could she despise a man so much, and still feel this disturbing attraction, this tingling awareness? Did he make all women feel this way? He had certainly demolished Stephanie's defences...and she was a sophisticated woman of the world, who had sworn to put her career before men and marriage. And now look at her, Calli pondered with a shiver. She's still reeling from what this man has done to her... She might never get over the way he savagely rejected her.

It was a relief when they passed into the modern bottling plant, where there were plenty of staff around and a friendly exchange of greetings to take her mind off her

sister—and the effect Armand Broch was having on her.
From there Armand led her into the pleasant wine-
tasting-room to meet his sister Leila. The room was
crowded with visitors clustering round the counter, selecting wines before closing time, while others were sitting
at long tables still sipping glasses of wine.

Leila and her helpers were too busy to do more than
smile a welcome at Calli as she passed through with
Armand. Calli was left with an impression of intelligent
brown eyes in a narrow, pleasant face, and dark hair
pulled smoothly back into a long pony-tail.

'You'll meet Leila properly later on,' Armand said as
they made their way outside. 'Now we'll go and find
Hamish.'

They found Leila's husband in the winery's well-
equipped quality-control laboratory. Calli was surprised
when Armand knocked before going in. She had expected him, as the big boss, to walk straight in. But
perhaps, by showing his staff respect, that was how he
had won their respect in return—and it had been apparent everywhere they went that he was a well-liked and
well-respected boss. Still, she mused cynically, she'd
known many men who conducted their businesses with
more integrity than they conducted their private lives.

'Got a moment to meet our new house guest?' Armand
asked his brother-in-law as they walked in.

'Sure.' Hamish's pale blue eyes were friendly as he
hastened over to shake Calli's hand, but the moment the
introductions were over Armand plucked her away,
muttering, 'We won't stop now, Hamish. You can say
a proper hello in the morning.'

'Hamish is a former chemist,' Armand informed her
as they left. 'He's very well-qualified, and full of bright

ideas. And dedicated, too. He'll keep on working, even in his own time.'

'You seem lucky in your staff,' Calli said spontaneously.

'Yes... they're very loyal,' said Armand, and there was a self-satisfied note in his voice that brought Calli's eyes round sharply. And discreet too, you're saying, she thought, tight-lipped, her opinion of him tumbling again. You're so confident, aren't you, Armand Broch, that they won't spill the beans about your personal behaviour to a nosy journalist? Well, we'll see...

As they emerged into the fresh air the huge ball of the sun was dipping towards the distant hills, and the sky was tinged with orange streaks. Calli was conscious of a curious warmth seeping through her. Everybody she had met so far, give or take the odd sideways glance, had been welcoming and friendly, even though this was obviously a busy time.

Her feeling of well-being followed her across the flag-stoned courtyard, where the sun, even now, was warm on her back and her senses were assailed by the sweet heady scent of ripe grapes and her head buzzed with pleasant sounds...the sound of laughter floating up from the rows of yellow-tipped vines as the pickers packed up for the day, the chirruping of birds in the gold-flecked branches, the drone of a truck bearing its load of grapes... Cheery sounds that echoed across the valley.

Her gaze hovered on the vine-clad slopes. No wonder Stephanie had loved it here... At the thought of her sister a twinge riffled through her, part guilt, part pain. If the Broch household knew that she was Stephanie's sister, would they be so welcoming then?

She sighed, wishing she felt more at ease about working here under false pretences. Because, strictly speaking, that was precisely what she was doing…putting on a pretence. Calling herself Caroline Barr Smith as though it were the name she used all the time. Not mentioning that Stephanie Fox was her sister. Hiding the fact that she intended to expose Armand Broch if she could. She hated deceiving people. Deceiving people she liked was doubly distasteful. And she felt she *was* going to like these people. Despite Armand Broch. Did he have any guilt feelings of his own? She very much doubted it!

'Well, now…' Armand glanced at his watch, looking anything *but* guilty '…you've seen just about everything now, except for our private cellar under the château. We have a superb collection of wines there for our own use; not just our own wines but the best from all over the world. I like to drink widely so as not to get used to my own faults. It's quite an incredible cellar… It was started by my grandfather.'

She stole a glance at his profile, allowing her eyes to stray up the strong column of his throat to the deep cleft in his chin, the lean cheekbones, the rather arrogant slash of his nose, noting that the cynical line down his cheek was not so marked now. As her eyes met his—their unusual green startling her anew—he gave her a sloping grin.

'Well, what do you think of our little world of wine and sunshine?' he asked with gentle mockery. 'Think you're going to enjoy your week here?'

Enjoy? She gave a guilty start. She hadn't come here to *enjoy* …or to fall under Armand Broch's indubitable spell, which no doubt he expected all women in his orbit to do. With a toss of her fair head she answered coolly, 'I'm sure I'm going to enjoy my…assignment,' laying a subtle stress on the word.

'Excellent,' he said smoothly, and the tiny gold flecks round the green irises glinted with amusement. 'I have a feeling we're going to get on famously.'

Calli felt a weakening in her knees, and with a frantic sense of self-preservation she deliberately conjured up her sister's anguished face—anguish that *this man* had caused. Armand Broch is a dangerous, ruthless man, Calli Smith, she reminded herself fiercely. And be it on your own head if you ever forget it!

CHAPTER FOUR

ARMAND BROCH was a man of his word—in some things at least—Calli discovered on that very first day. When she went up to her room after Armand had taken his leave of her she found a bowl of yellow roses on the dressing-table. A small gesture on his part, but it surprised and pleased her. She hadn't expected him to remember that off-the-cuff promise he had made earlier, after she had told him how much she loved roses.

This is the way he gets around a woman, she told herself sternly, resolutely burying her initial pleasure. He wants to butter you up so that you'll write nice things about him. The Armand Brochs of this world never do anything without a purpose—or without some personal gain in mind, she concluded with a tightening of her lips.

She was, she realised, beginning to feel quite droopy with fatigue. The long drive from Melbourne and her early-morning start were finally catching up with her. It was tempting, knowing that Armand and his sister and brother-in-law were all going to be out for the evening, to find a way to steal down into Armand's private cellar, in the chance that she might be able to find Stephanie's lost diamond. But she quickly rejected the idea. A cellar as valuable as that was bound to be kept locked and bolted, and she had no idea where to start looking for a key. Besides which she would have no excuse to offer if she was caught prowling around down there on her very first night. Anyway, Agnes was still around—she

had said she would be up shortly with her tea—and
Armand would no doubt expect the woman to keep an
eye on the new house guest and make sure she didn't
make off with the family silver. He had very markedly
given Calli a TV guide and pointed out that she had a
television set in her room, which she could watch before
retiring. He obviously expected her to stay put this
evening, and grab her chance to have an early night.

She yawned widely. And that was precisely what she
intended to do. There were bound to be other opportunities during the week, and by then she should know
her way round a bit better. Perhaps they would even trust
her enough to give her the run of the château!

Though that, of course, was a bit too much to expect!

Breakfast, as Armand had told her the night before, was
at seven-thirty on the dot—it was going to be a busy
Monday because he had a string of appointments in
town. Heeding the warning, she made sure she showed
up in the breakfast-room off the kitchen dead on time.
She had her camera slung over her shoulder as she
strolled into the room.

Three sets of eyes widened in dismay.

'You're going to snap that thing at us while we eat
our breakfast?' Armand's tanned brow lowered ominously, while Hamish and Leila swapped disconcerted
looks.

'Only this morning,' she assured them hastily.
'Breakfast in a typical week in the life of Armand Broch.
You don't mind?' She flashed a smile at him.

Something flickered in his eyes, as if her smile, or
something about it, had caught him by surprise. She
realised it was the first real smile she had given him since
she had arrived. 'A deal's a deal, I guess,' he said with

a resigned sigh. 'I did agree to this caper. OK, get it over with. And then you can eat too.'

He was more formally dressed this morning, in a crisp white business shirt and a sober tie, and his dark hair was neatly combed and still slightly damp from his shower. Her own pleated navy skirt and demure white blouse seemed appropriate, as did the way she was wearing her hair, brushed back into a businesslike coil behind.

Over breakfast the talk, during this extremely busy vintage time, was mostly to do with grape quality and winemaking. Calli suspected that the family was deliberately avoiding touching on anything personal, or even anything too specific about the business side of things, because there was an outsider present—and, worse, a journalist. At least it meant they weren't probing into her own personal life or background! But she did make one attempt to draw them out about the movie which had been filmed on location here, simply to test the water.

'Oh, that!' Leila pulled a face. 'We were glad to see them all go. What with one thing and another.'

When she didn't elucidate Calli said lightly, 'It must have been interesting, though—seeing how a film is made, and having movie stars staying under your roof. Are they as temperamental as people claim?'

She hoped that this would lead to some mention of Stephanie, and perhaps even Roxy Manning, the supporting actress who had lured Armand away from Stephanie. She was watching Armand's face from beneath her thick lashes as Hamish answered with a shrug, 'They're really not much different from anyone else when they're not acting a part. The trouble is,' he gave an ironic grin, 'they tend to go on acting a part, even after the shooting stops.'

'What do you mean?' Calli asked, her eyes veering away from Armand's impassive features.

Hamish shrugged. 'Oh, you know what the acting profession is like...' She saw him glance briefly at Armand.

'If you'll excuse me,' Armand said, pushing back his chair. 'I have a full day ahead. Caroline, if you intend to come to town with me I'd like to leave in ten minutes.'

Calli leapt up at once. 'I'll be ready.' Questions would have to wait for some other time. Perhaps one night over dinner, when tongues had been loosened by some of Château Broch's fine wines... and preferably at a time, if she could wangle it, when Armand was occupied elsewhere.

But before any of them could leave the room they heard a door bang shut, and scuffling sounds coming from the kitchen, accompanied by a flurry of voices, and a moment later Agnes appeared in the doorway, clasping her hands in agitation.

Armand frowned. 'What's up, Agnes?'

'There's been an accident. One of the pickers... he's cut off the top of his finger. It—it's dangling by a thread.'

'Where is he?'

'In the kitchen. They're packing it in ice. Ben's all set to take him to the local hospital, but the lad—Tom Rattle, his name is—he's worried stiff about what's going to happen to his finger. He plays in a band, you see——'

'OK, Agnes, I'll handle it. Caroline!' Armand snapped over his shoulder. 'Be ready to leave as soon as I've made some phone calls.'

As Armand vanished into the kitchen Calli flew upstairs to grab her notebook and jacket, pausing only to clean her teeth and freshen up her lipstick. When she came down Armand was already at the car, settling young Tom Rattle into the back seat. The young man was nursing a bandaged hand, and looked very white-faced. But he seemed to have calmed down, and was sitting quietly.

'I'm taking him to a hospital in town,' Armand told Calli briefly. 'You sit in the back with him. Keep an eye on him. But no photographs!'

'No, of course not.' As she slipped into the back seat the injured young man gave her a weak smile.

'I don't mind if you take photographs,' he said gamely. 'You make sure you write this up. Mr Broch has been great—he's arranged for the best microsurgeon in town to operate on my finger. Fancy! Says he'll have it as good as new!'

'That's wonderful,' said Calli, smiling back.

Tom leaned towards her, dropping his voice as Armand settled into the front seat and revved the engine. 'Mr Broch says I'm not to worry about a thing—he'll pay for everything! He's a terrific boss. Anyone else would have dumped me at the local hospital and let me take pot luck!'

Calli fell silent as the car took off smoothly and gradually gathered speed. Hearing such fulsome praise about the man she wanted to expose as being totally heartless, lacking any redeeming qualities, had rather thrown her.

Of course, a man could be a pillar of virtue in his professional life, and still be a louse when it came to his relationships with women, she consoled herself. Let's just see if he can keep his halo intact for a full week! I'll lay odds he can't!

On the drive into town Armand kept young Tom's attention away from himself by talking about the won-

derful vintage it was going to be this year, about how
pleased he was with his pickers this season, about more
or less anything that would uplift the ailing young man
rather than plunge him into gloomy introspection.

Calli had to concede grudgingly that his efforts were
paying off. By the time they reached the hospital in the
heart of Adelaide colour was already seeping back into
Tom's cheeks, and he insisted that Calli take his photograph as Armand was helping him from the car. At
Calli's enquiring glance Armand nodded briefly, and she
raised her camera and caught Tom's trusting smile.

Armand insisted on staying with Tom until the microsurgeon arrived—in fact, right up until the moment Tom
was wheeled into the operating theatre. Then he took
some extra time contacting Tom's parents and explaining what had happened, and only left the hospital
when he was assured that they were on their way.

The rest of the day passed swiftly, as Armand's appointments had to be sandwiched into the remaining
hours, with little breathing-space between. First there
was an appointment with the marketing and sales
manager of a radio station, where variations of
Armand's new advertising jingle were played, so that he
could decide which one would be used on air during the
coming weeks.

As Armand made his decision Calli's pen flew over
her notebook, and her camera was kept busy until they
moved on to their next appointment, with Adelaide's
top tailor. An advertising man met them there. Armand
was to appear in full-page advertisements for his
favourite suits, having been included in a recent list of
Australia's top ten best-dressed men. They discussed a
catchy introduction to accompany the screed on Armand,

and when that was decided they made an appointment
to come back the next day.

'Now...we have time for a quick lunch,' Armand said,
and drove her to his restaurant on the banks of the
Torrens River. On the way he rang the hospital on his
car phone and was told that Tom Rattle was out of
surgery and his parents had already taken him home.
His finger had been saved, and they expected him to
regain full use of it in time. 'Thanks...that's great news.'

As they walked into the restaurant they were met by
the proprietor, a tall striking woman with red hair cut
in a smooth bob.

'Davina!' Armand's green eyes softened as he bent to
kiss her on the cheek.

Davina? Calli's eyes widened, and then narrowed. The
woman he had been speaking to on the telephone yesterday? 'I *need* you, sweetheart,' he had breathed into
the phone. And he had rushed off to spend the evening
with her, intending to ply her with champagne and be
'very persuasive'. Persuading her into his bed—where
else? Pursing her lips, Calli raised her camera and
snapped.

Armand's head whipped round. 'For goodness' sake,
Caroline, put that damned thing away and let me relax
for once. Davina, my pet, this is Caroline...the journalist
I was telling you about.' His tone was dry.

'My, you certainly know how to pick them, Armand,'
Davina commented, raising her eyebrows a fraction as
she ran her eyes over Calli's shining fair hair and small
oval face. Surely she couldn't be jealous? Calli thought,
flushing. Not of me. 'You be careful, Caroline, dear,'
Davina warned her in an undertone as she caught Calli's
arm and ushered her ahead of Armand to a table over-
looking the river. 'You're so young! And Armand is a

dangerously attractive man. For your own preservation, darling, I wouldn't go getting any ideas...'

She's warning me off... Calli blinked in surprise. As if she need worry about competition from me. Even if I were smitten, which is a laugh, she'd be safe. Davina is *gorgeous*.

'Don't worry, I won't,' she promised fervently.

'What are you two whispering about?' Armand demanded from behind.

'Just girl talk, darling,' Davina said, and laughed a rich throaty laugh. 'I'm afraid I'm going to have to leave you,' she apologised, glancing past them. 'There's a big party just arriving. It's going to be a busy day.'

'Off you go,' Armand said easily. 'I'll catch up later.' He looked at her meaningfully, and Davina actually flushed.

'You're making it very difficult for me, Armand Broch,' she breathed softly, as she hastened away.

Was she playing hard to get? Refusing to go to bed with him? Calli kept her face impassive as she sat down.

Armand didn't enlighten her. Naturally. He wouldn't want his personal setbacks appearing in her feature article!

The dining-room was abuzz with lunchtime diners, mostly businessmen, but service was quick and efficient, and their seafood crêpes were exquisite. Armand wasn't in a chatty mood. His gaze kept straying, and Calli realised he was following Davina about the room, a moody expression in his eyes. Was he planning his next move? It obviously wasn't the right time to start quizzing him about anything. His mind was elsewhere.

After the light meal Armand ordered cappuccinos for both of them, and as they were sipping them the early-afternoon sun suddenly streamed across the table—

beaming directly into Calli's face. As she raised a hand
to shade her eyes against the glare she noticed that
Armand was staring at her, as if he'd just noticed her
for the first time. When he didn't glance away as her
eyes met his she felt herself flushing, and then, angry at
herself for blushing like a schoolgirl, for reacting at all,
especially to *this* man, she frowned and asked evenly,
'Do I have spinach between my teeth?'

His eyes flickered with amused irony. 'I was admiring
those lovely grey eyes of yours. With the sunlight on
them they're as bright as polished pewter. Clear, candid,
expressive eyes, and yet—so full of hidden depths...'

She let her lashes sweep down immediately, at the same
time realising to her annoyance that her flush had
deepened.

'Are you sure you're not an imposter, Caroline Barr
Smith?' he murmured softly.

Her lashes whipped up again. 'An...imposter?
Wh-what do you mean?' Had he seen some resemblance
to Stephanie after all? Had he guessed who she was?

His expression was unreadable as he answered
smoothly, 'You don't strike me as being the usual run-
of-the-mill journalist, Caroline. From my experience,
they're hard-boiled, pushy, insensitive creatures with
strident voices and no consideration. And they certainly
don't blush! The journalists I've known would have
seized the chance to grill me over lunch. But you seemed
to realise I didn't want to talk, that I needed time to
think...'

She was so relieved that he hadn't guessed who she
was that her lips burst into a smile. And a tiny shock
flew through her as his expression changed, his eyes
flaring for a moment, enhancing the green, before his
own lips stretched into an answering smile—the kind of

smile that would dissolve steel, Calli thought, trying her hardest not to be affected by it. If he had ever smiled at Stephanie like that no wonder she had fallen so hard for him. Calli thanked her lucky stars that she knew the heartless brute that lay behind that devastating smile, or she might have been in grave danger of falling for him herself!

'What made you decide to become a journalist?' he asked, the deep, attractive timbre of his voice making it even harder to withstand him, to maintain her antagonism.

'I rather fell into it,' she admitted with a shrug. 'I really wanted to be a writer...I've been scribbling stories all my life. But writing stories doesn't pay the bills when you're an unknown, so I applied for a cadetship at the *Melbourne Star*, and eventually I was lucky enough to get one. I also did a photography course, to give me a second string to my bow. That's why I do my own camera work.'

'And are you still writing stories?'

'When I have the time,' she said. 'I'd love to be able to write whenever I want to, but——' She stopped, clamping her teeth down over her lip. Armand Broch didn't want to hear all this. The daydreams of a silly journalist! You'll have him thinking you don't care about your work, you dimwit!

'We'd better move on,' Armand said, pushing back his chair. His tone was apologetic rather than bored. Or was he just being polite? 'Coming?'

She nodded, and reached for her handbag and camera. Before leaving the restaurant Armand rang Château Broch and passed on the good news about Tom, and from there they drove to Armand's central office in town, where he had a meeting with his sales representatives.

During the meeting Calli took a couple of photographs and jotted down Armand's comments in her notebook.

'I want our wines on every wine list in every restaurant in the country. No excuses.'

The talk went back and forth across the table. Armand made it clear that what he wanted to see in his representatives were good old-fashioned qualities like loyalty, honesty, politeness—'We don't rubbish other products'—and hard work. He dismissed negative attitudes as unhealthy, and praised anyone who came up with constructive criticism. And, above all, he made it clear that he relished a questioning, flexible mind.

Despite herself, Calli was impressed.

If he only employed those same qualities in his private life, she thought with a sigh, one could almost admire the man.

During a coffee break halfway through the meeting she overheard one of the reps remark to another, 'Armand wouldn't be Armand without a pretty girl in tow,' and heard the other reply,

'Lucky devil. D'you reckon he'll ever stop playing the field and settle down?'

'Why should he? When he can snap his fingers and have a gorgeous bird whenever he wants one? He attracts them like moths to a flame. Doesn't even have to chase them. He just takes what's on offer.'

Calli turned her head sharply. Surely they didn't think that *she* ... that *he* ...?

The one nearest to her caught her eye and had the grace to look discomfited. He said quickly, leaning towards her, 'I wasn't inferring that you were one of Armand's—er——'

The other man nudged him. 'You're only making it worse, Raymond. To listen to you, anyone would think

Armand had a whole harem of women. At least give the man credit for only having one woman at a time.' That's how little you know, thought Calli, but she said nothing as the other nodded and said with a sigh of envy,

'I guess he can't help it if women are forever throwing themselves at him.'

Raymond chuckled. 'One of these days he'll be smitten by a girl who *won't* fall at his feet. And if he wants her badly enough he'll have to do the chasing himself—a new experience for Armand, I imagine.'

'She'll have to be someone pretty special to hold on to Armand,' said the other. 'There'll always be other women panting for him...tempting him...trying to lure him away. Can you see him turning his back on them for long?'

'You might be surprised. His type usually fall the hardest *when* they finally fall.'

'Maybe. But I can't see it happening in the foreseeable future. He's having too good a time.'

Raymond stroked his chin. 'I wonder. Strikes me he's a man who's looking for something...and just hasn't found it yet.'

The meeting was called to order and the two men excused themselves and drifted back to the table to take their places. Calli pulled out her notebook and thoughtfully jotted down what she could remember of the conversation, wondering with faint cynicism if it could be true—that Armand would give up playing the field if he could only find the right woman.

Rot, she sniffed. She thought of Stephanie, who had loved him to distraction, and wondered cynically what sentiments had motivated Armand in that particular relationship. If Armand had only wanted to play around, why had he gone as far as asking her to marry him? It wasn't as if her sister had never had an affair before, or had been playing hard to get. Stephanie had been crazy about him, and she was a woman of experience—she wouldn't need a marriage proposal before she gave in to a man if she wanted him enough.

Unless... Calli chewed on her lip. Unless her sister had been so besotted with Armand Broch that she wouldn't settle for anything less than marriage. Had she coaxed him, *forced* him into proposing... never realising that he was the sort of man who would promise anything to get a woman into his bed?

She shook her head. Just what kind of man *was* Armand Broch to fool the woman who loved him in such a despicable way? If another woman were to come along now, would he toss aside Davina the way he had tossed aside Stephanie—and, by the look of it, Roxy Manning too? Armand had talked of loyalty today to his representatives. Was his own loyalty to others only skin deep? Did he confine it solely to his business dealings?

On the drive back to the Barossa Valley the traffic was heavy, and Armand, hunched over the wheel, was not communicative. It had been a long day, and he seemed to have a lot on his mind. Davina, no doubt, being uppermost.

Calli made no attempt to intrude. She had quite enough of her own to think about.

Twilight was falling when they reached the vine-covered slopes of the Barossa Valley, and as they were driving through the small town of Lyndoch, not far from Château Broch, Armand's car phone rang. Rather than pull into the kerb, he switched his microphone on, and Leila's worried voice filled the interior of the car.

'Armand, where are you?'

'Just leaving Lyndoch. What's up?'

'Bill Dysan's had a bad car accident. His wife just rang me from the Flinders Hospital. They were flown into town by helicopter.'

Calli felt Armand tense beside her. 'Is he badly hurt?'

'Afraid so. Severe chest injuries. Broken bones. It's touch and go. Yvonne sounded terribly upset.'

'Is anyone with her?'

'I don't think so. They don't have any family in South Australia.'

'Where's Kurt? Why isn't he with her?'

'No one knows where he is. He left work early and must have taken Amy and their girls out somewhere. They're not answering their phone.'

Armand swore under his breath. 'Pack me a bag, Leila. I'm going back to town. We'll stay the night.' He glanced at Calli, and said with a faint sigh, 'Get Agnes to pack a bag for Caroline too. A few toiletries and a nightie or whatever. We'll be home in a few minutes. We'll just grab what we need and leave straight away.'

'Armand, you can't drive all the way back to town now,' Leila protested. 'You'll be exhausted. And you haven't had any dinner. They're doing all they can. Can't you wait until morning?'

'Morning might be too late. Yvonne needs me now. Make sure those things are ready for us.' Armand cut off the connection.

Calli looked at him sympathetically. 'A close friend of yours?' she asked softly.

'An employee. He works for Kurt at our McLaren Vale vineyard. Bill's a good man. A good worker too.'

Despite her own private feelings for Armand, Calli felt a new grudging respect for him. Not a friend. Not even one of Armand's own employees. An employee of his brother Kurt. And yet Armand was going to turn around and drive all the way back to Adelaide to check on the man personally and comfort his anxious wife.

And he was going to take her with him. Not because he wanted to, she realised that. He was taking her because that was the arrangement—she was to accompany him wherever he went this week. She fingered her chin thoughtfully. Where were they going to stay overnight? Would Armand, after they had visited the hospital, book her into a room somewhere, leave her there, and then disappear—to see Davina?

Or...she flushed...would he put his pursuit of Davina behind him for this evening, and stay with *her*? Calli pictured herself alone with Armand in the same hotel...just the two of them, together, and felt the warmth in her cheeks deepen. Would Armand Broch, notorious womaniser that she knew him to be, try to take advantage of the situation? Would he book adjoining rooms, perhaps, in the hope that——?

She felt a suffocating sensation, as if the air were being crushed from her, just as the grapes in the big presses were crushed of their juices.

What are you panicking for? she scolded herself. He's not going to try anything. Even if he does, you can handle it. You know the kind of man he is. And forewarned, they say, is forearmed...

CHAPTER FIVE

ON THE long drive back to Adelaide they munched the sandwiches which Agnes had hurriedly prepared for them, and afterwards Calli found herself nodding off, her head lolling to one side.

'You can wake up now—we're here.' Armand's amused voice, close to her ear, jolted her awake, and her cheeks flamed when she opened her eyes and realised she had her head on his shoulder!

She scrambled upright, mumbling an apology.

'My pleasure,' he drawled. He swung the car into a vacant car park. 'Want to come in with me?'

She nodded. 'Would you mind if I bring my camera? I promise I won't intrude.'

He studied her face for a moment, and then nodded. 'No...I don't think you will. Come along, then.'

Bill Dysan's wife Yvonne, her thin face tense with anxiety, met them outside Intensive Care.

'Mr Broch! How kind of you to——'

'Armand...please. Have you heard how Bill is?' Armand touched her arm as he spoke, and Calli, watching from behind, had the strangest feeling that she was actually witnessing Armand's strength flowing from his fingers into the woman's arm, comforting her trembling.

'They're operating,' Yvonne said worriedly. 'He's been in there for ages.'

'He's in good hands,' Armand said, his hand still on her arm. 'I'll stay with you, Yvonne. You won't be alone.'

'Oh, thank you, Mr Br...Armand. I really do appreciate it.'

While they were both standing close together, Yvonne's eyes moist with gratitude as she looked up at Armand, Armand towering over her, strong and comforting, Calli raised her camera—only to lower it again without taking a shot. She would have to use her flashlight, she realised, and it struck her that it might appear callous, popping lights at such a moment. Instead she stored the moment away in her memory. What she couldn't describe in pictures she could always describe in words.

Armand turned his head at that moment, and his gaze caught hers. His expression seemed to soften, as if he was silently thanking her for her consideration, and then he beckoned her forward and introduced her to Yvonne.

'Caroline, why don't you go and find some coffee? I'll sit here with Yvonne until we have some news on Bill.'

She nodded. 'You could do with some too,' she said, eyeing the lines of strain in his face and the dark smudges under his eyes. He had done a lot of driving today, on top of a busy day. And now this. 'I'll fetch some for both of you.'

It was another hour and a half before they had any news. The chief surgeon himself came out and spoke to Yvonne. He had the sister in charge with him.

'He's out of danger,' he told her, and Calli saw Yvonne's shoulders slump in relief—and noted that Armand was right there beside her with a supporting hand at her elbow. 'You can see him for just a moment. Then I want him to sleep. You could do with some too, I'd say, Mrs Dysan. I've arranged for you to have a room here for the night.'

'Oh, thank you, thank you,' Yvonne whispered, seizing the surgeon's hand. She turned to Armand. 'Thank you so much, Armand, for staying with me. I'll be fine now.'

'Tell Bill he's not to worry about a thing,' Armand said, the harsh lines in his cheeks easing into a smile. 'He's just to concentrate on getting better. I'll be staying in town tonight, and will come and see him in the morning. If you should need me in the meantime you can ring me at this number.' He thrust a piece of paper into her hand.

Yvonne thanked him again, and disappeared into the intensive-care ward with the sister in charge.

'Coming?' Armand asked Calli, and as they left the hospital he commented, 'You didn't take any photos.'

'No.'

'I'm sure Yvonne appreciated it.' He didn't say it, but she sensed that he did too, and for some reason she was glad she hadn't disappointed him. 'Let's get to the motel and have a nightcap. I need one. Don't you?'

Her heart gave a tiny jump. *Motel*, he'd said. Motels didn't normally have bars. Did he mean... in his room? And just what did he have in mind when he'd suggested a nightcap? She felt hot needles prickling her scalp. If she said yes, what would she be saying yes *to*?

Somehow she kept her tone light as she asked warily, 'That could depend on what you mean by a nightcap.'

She saw amusement flicker in his eyes. And something else. Surprise? Or, more likely... frustration!

'Just a drink to soothe our weary nerves,' he spelt out with a smile. A smile that reached his eyes, accentuating the gold flecks in the green.

She relaxed. 'A drink, by all means. I could do with one too.'

'Then shall we go?' He proffered his arm, but she moved on, pretending not to notice. What was it she was afraid of? she wondered ruefully as they headed back to the car. Of him? Knowing how he had treated women in the past, she had good reason to be wary. But somewhere deep down she knew that what she feared even more than Armand was her own possible response. There was something compellingly attractive about Armand Broch—a dangerous magnetism, more potent than she had encountered in any other man—and, much as she despised him for what he had done to her sister, she'd be a fool to imagine herself immune, untouched by it. Silly to take any risks. Best simply to stay at a safe distance.

The motel wasn't far from the hospital, and in no time they were booked in and putting their bags into adjoining rooms. Calli noticed that there was a connecting door between her room and his, and her heart began to beat a rat-tat-tat in her chest. Was it kept locked? She wasn't game to try it, for fear that Armand, on the other side, would hear and wonder what she was up to, or perhaps even...get ideas.

'Fool,' she chided herself. 'He just wants to unwind over a drink, and then we'll go to bed. *Separately.* He's not going to get involved with the journalist who's doing a write-up on him. He's not that stupid.'

Just to make sure she cautiously moved a table to one side, sliding it silently along the carpet so that it partially obstructed the adjoining door. That done, she giggled, and shook her head.

'You poor dope. He won't even try the door. He doesn't have any designs on you...Armand Broch isn't a man to mix business with pleasure.'

Isn't he just? an irritating voice mocked her. Isn't he involved in some way with Davina, the woman who runs his restaurant by the river? Doesn't he have his secretary Lauren to stay the night occasionally, when she acts as hostess for him?

She gave a hiccup of nervous laughter.

And then jumped, hearing a knock at her door. Not her *outer* door, but the door between their rooms!

'Caroline, are you ready for that drink?' Armand called out. 'Come on in. Your room key should unlock this door.'

She gasped back, 'There—there's something in front of the door, blocking it. I—I'll come the other way.' There was no way she was going to shift that table again, and make that connecting doorway a handy little thoroughfare!

She caught sight of her face in the mirror as she darted for the outer door, and grimaced when she saw her flushed cheeks and over-bright eyes. Oh, hell, she thought . . . what am I getting myself into?

She threw open the outside door—and almost bowled straight into Armand's arms!

'Wh—what are you doing?' she shrilled, pulling up sharply. 'I thought——'

'I was just coming in to move that obstruction.' His gaze flickered past her, and she felt her cheeks burning as he noted the table that was partially blocking the connecting door between their rooms. Would he guess that she had moved it there herself?

He looked amused. Not dangerous—just amused.

'Well, OK,' he said, turning back. 'Come this way, if you'd rather.'

She hastened past him, burningly aware of the whimsical smile on his lips as he followed her into his room and closed the door behind him.

'What can I get you to drink?' he asked, turning to the small refrigerator. 'Brandy? Scotch?'

'I'll have a brandy and dry, thanks. A weak one.'

'Ice?'

'Yes, please.' The weaker the better!

When he had poured her drink and a Scotch for himself he waved her to a chair and lowered himself into the armchair opposite. Calli would have loved to have kicked off her shoes, but she didn't dare. He might get the idea that she was making herself comfortable...putting out feelers—to him!

'Cheers,' Armand said, breaking the silence.

'Cheers.' Calli raised her drink and sipped long and slowly, enjoying the icy coolness as it slid down her throat. She sat back with a sigh. She was starting to feel better already.

'It's been a long, exhausting day for you...for your first day on the job,' Armand remarked, his gaze sweeping lazily over her face. 'You have been very patient...and very thoughtful; not at all intrusive. I appreciate it.'

His praise warmed her—or was it the brandy? 'It's been quite a day for you too,' she returned, finding it easier to talk to him than she would have imagined only seconds ago. 'Two unexpected hospital visits, on top of your normal schedule. But I suppose you're used to packing a lot into your day.'

'To life in the fast lane, you mean?' he mocked gently. 'I guess so. But it's always good to relax too, when I get the chance. Especially after a day like this one. And I find I can relax with you, Caroline. There are not too many women who can make me feel that way. Most women are forever hectoring a guy for attention, or reassurance, or some such thing. But you, Caroline…there's a calmness about you that I find very comforting, especially right now, when, quite frankly, I feel pooped. Not,' he added hastily, as Calli's lips parted, 'that I find you boring, or unalluring. Hell, nothing could be further from the truth!'

She shifted uncomfortably in her chair. Armand was watching her in a manner that did nothing to help the way she felt. She let her eyelids flutter downward, masking her eyes. She didn't know that, in the glow of the gold-shaded lamp above her, her clear skin had taken on a breath-catching translucence, her wide, faintly tilted eyes had turned a deeper, more incandescent grey, and her soft fair hair danced with subtle gold highlights.

'You're a beautiful woman, Caroline.'

At his words a deep reaction pulsed through her. Steeling herself against his flattery, she raised her chin and eyed him sceptically, without encouragement. She didn't want that kind of talk from Armand Broch. She mustn't listen to it. It was just a line…just words. Words he'd used a thousand times before, to a thousand different women.

'I've embarrassed you. I'm sorry.'

'Not at all.' She spoke more sharply than she had intended. Embarrassed? What did he think she was—a naïve young thing just out of school, to be embarrassed by a man's compliments? 'I just don't care much for idle flattery.'

'You think that's what it was?' He was looking amused now, a faintly baffled crease appearing between the dark brows. 'What is it about you, Caroline Barr Smith, that makes you so...intriguingly different from other women? I can't quite make you out.'

She couldn't let this go on. It was getting too personal. Dangerously personal.

'Armand, tell me about the movie that was filmed at Château Broch,' she urged, her eyelashes sweeping down as she took another sip of her drink. A longer sip this time. '*The Winemaker*, they've called it, haven't they?'

'Why do I get the impression you don't want to talk about yourself?' Armand said, faintly teasing. 'OK, then...but I don't see what that movie has to do with the article you're writing.'

Her gaze flickered up again. 'Oh, it has nothing to do with it,' she said lightly. 'Look, no notebook. I just thought it was a...' She shrugged.

'A nice, safe topic? Safer than talking about yourself?'

She managed a grin. 'Well, a harmless enough topic for the end of a long day.'

'Hm.' He was eyeing her speculatively, the tiny gold flecks in his eyes flickering like sunlight dancing on a green sea. 'All right, then, I'll tell you as much as I know. In a nutshell, a bored Sydney socialite, played by Stephanie Fox, inherits a winery from her uncle, and decides to give up her idle life and run it herself. The winemaker, played by Australian heart-throb Larry Nicholls, doesn't think much of his new boss. He's convinced her decision is just a whim, a passing fancy she'll grow tired of—if she doesn't ruin the place first. The sparks fly. The winemaker's girlfriend, played by Roxy Manning, watches the sparks gradually turn to passion as the heroine shows she's got the grit to stay and make it work. She becomes insanely jealous, and tries to ruin the heroine by starting a fire, and when that fails she tries to kill her.'

Calli ran her tongue along suddenly dry lips. Had the emotions on the set been echoed in real life? Had Roxy Manning been insanely jealous of Stephanie *off* the set as well—either professionally or personally—and was that why she had come between Stephanie and Armand?

She gave a trembling sigh, and as Armand paused for breath she hazarded, 'I understand there was some real-life rivalry between Roxy Manning and Stephanie Fox...'

'Was there?' He looked surprised. Then he shrugged and said, 'Well, I guess there could have been. Larry and Stephanie played some rather sizzling love scenes on the set. I suppose they could have made Roxy jealous.'

Calli blinked. Roxy Manning had been jealous of *Larry* and Stephanie? 'But...why?' She forced the question out.

'Because Roxy was crazy about Larry—she made no secret of it.'

Calli stared at him. Roxy had been playing around with Larry Nicholls *as well as* Armand? No wonder Stephanie had called her a slut!

Roxy Manning and Armand Broch are as bad as each other, she fumed inwardly. Neither of them cares who they hurt!

'Caroline, I wish I knew what was going on inside that busy little head of yours!' Armand's voice broke into her thoughts, his voice a low rumble, his tone faintly perplexed.

Calli raised her drink to her lips and gulped down the remains. 'Nothing. What makes you think...? Look, it really is time I went to bed,' she said, wanting only to escape now. 'I'm feeling so tired...I can't think straight.'

'Bed...ah, yes, that sounds good.'

There was an inflexion in his voice that sent a hot little shiver tracing over her skin. Her heart seemed suddenly

to seize up in her chest, and desperately she tried to quell
the images that leapt into her mind, images that caused
her heart to race and sent waves of hot blood pulsating
through her. Why was he having this astonishing effect
on her... this man she despised above all other men?
She mustn't think about him... not in that way... not
in any way!

*Remember Stephanie... remember how he hurt your
sister!*

Icy reality washed over her, keeping her sane until she
reached the door and swung it open, mumbling, 'Goodnight, Armand!' before she plunged outside, to gulp in
the fresh night air. She had barely reached the door of
her own room when she realised that Armand had followed her, and was standing over her, tall and far too
close, as she fumbled for her key. Chokingly aware of
the musky aftershave still clinging to his skin, she felt a
wave of light-headedness, as if she had been drinking all
evening rather than sipping just one weak brandy,
watered down with ice and dry ginger ale.

'You're to sleep in in the morning, Caroline,' Armand
said sternly. 'I'll order a hot breakfast to be brought to
your room. While you're having it I'll nip out and see
Davina before she starts work for the day. You needn't
come. I won't be long. We'll go to the hospital about
nine-thirty to see Bill.'

So... he hadn't forgotten Davina. Why hadn't he gone
to see her tonight? Because she was on duty at the restaurant? Because it was too late and he was feeling too
tired? 'Pooped', he'd put it. It could hardly be because
he had wanted to stay here with her!

'Give me your key, Caroline.'

'I can manage——'

'Give it to me.'

He took the key from her trembling fingers and unlocked her door, and as she darted past him he followed
her, switching on the wall-lamp while she was still trying
to find the switch. She realised she was hardly breathing,
though her heart was making up for it, galloping like a
herd of wild horses. *Why had he followed her into her
room?*

He strode to the table and picked up one of the
breakfast menus. 'Right...what will you have? Fresh
orange juice? Cereal? Scrambled eggs and bacon? Or
would you prefer steak and eggs?'

'Eggs and bacon will be fine,' she gulped, relief
bursting through her. He only wanted her breakfast
order! 'And yes, orange juice. And tea. Thank you.'

'Right.' He wrote down her order and stepped towards
the door. Once there, he paused, and something in the
way he turned, his broad-shouldered body revolving
soundlessly, graceful for all his size and height, made
her breath catch in her throat. The strength seemed to
ebb from her body, and her pulse skittered alarmingly.

Armand looked at her for a long moment without
speaking. She realised she was hardly breathing, though
her heart was making up for it, almost jumping out of
her chest. For a long stunned moment there was so much
static between them that she thought the air must snap
with it.

'Goodnight, Caroline.' His voice seemed to rumble
right through her. And he had moved a step closer!

For a moment she couldn't trust herself to speak.
Every nerve-end in her body was conscious of the tall
taut body so close to her own, vibrating with masculinity as he watched her, the slide of his eyes down her
face and body like the brush of fingertips, arousing
pulses she didn't know she possessed; pulses that

throbbed in her neck, her wrists, her temple, and deep inside her body.

She became acutely aware of sounds drifting in from the street, the piercing wail of a siren, the steady drone of the traffic, the sharp squeal of tyres.

With a superhuman effort, summoning the last drop of her will-power, she managed to break the spell. 'Goodnight, Armand.' The words seemed to come from somewhere other than her own lips, and hang in the air above her.

His eyelids quivered, further shadowing his enigmatic gaze. Reaching out, he brushed her cheek lightly with his hand, his warm flesh only just touching her own so that the fine golden hairs on her skin tingled under his palm.

'I don't know what it is about you, Caroline Barr Smith. There's something... some quality——' He paused, shrugging. 'What is it, I wonder, that makes you different from other women I've known?'

She felt a tightness in her chest. What was it about *him* that was making her react the way she was, when she knew the kind of man he was, and hated him for it? And, as for his finding *her* different, she was well aware that she was not like Armand Broch's other women. She had none of Stephanie's bold dark beauty, none of Davina's smooth sophistication, none of the glitz and glamour of the other women in his life. No wonder he thought her 'different'. She wasn't his type at all!

As she averted her face in instinctive withdrawal the golden wash of the lamp on the wall shone full in her face. She heard him draw a sharp breath.

'You have a lovely face, Caroline. There's a purity about it... like crystal.'

Her eyes wavered under his. She hoped he couldn't hear the thumping in her chest, the erratic pounding in her ears. He was standing unbearably close, so close that she was vividly aware of the feverish brilliance of his eyes, the thick curve of his dark brows, the fullness of his mouth, the deep dark cleft in his chin.

She backed away, scepticism fighting other emotions she didn't dare examine. 'Intriguingly different', he had called her earlier. And now he was calling her 'lovely', and comparing her face to crystal!

They're just words to him, she thought fiercely. Meaningless platitudes. Words came easily to a man like Armand Broch. She didn't want to hear them. Especially not from the man who had a proven track record for hurting the women close to him. Hurting her own sister! Let him keep his facile flattery for the other women in his life. She didn't want to hear any more.

She swung round, away from him, her expression stonily impassive, her stormy eyes hidden from him.

'Caroline——'

He caught her arm, drawing an involuntary gasp from her. Her eyes leapt round, her breath strangling in her throat as she sensed the change in him. It was in the huskiness of his voice, in the urgent grip of his fingers, in the green flame in his eyes.

No...no...please... This time she made no attempt to hide the pleading in her eyes. *Please go.* She tried to utter the words aloud, but no sound came out.

'What are you afraid of, Caroline?' Armand asked quietly, peering into her face. 'Is it me? Or is it men in general?'

She managed to find her voice then. 'Of course I'm not afraid of men. Or of *you*.' It was nowhere near her normal voice, but at least she had succeeded in getting the words out!

'Suspicious, then? Caroline, you don't want to believe all the stories you've heard about me. They tend to be wildly exaggerated.'

Did they? She had heard from her sister's own lips just how Armand Broch treated his women. *Mistreated* them, rather! He was afraid she would tell the truth about him in her article... that was why he was saying all these things, why he was sweet-talking her.

'Caroline... I wasn't just doing a line. I meant every word. Can't you trust me?' pleaded the man she trusted least in all the world. She felt a suffocating sensation as he closed the gap between them, his eyes swimming over hers like an endless green sea, his hand sliding up her arm to cup her chin, tilting it upward, the touch of his fingertips like red-hot needles on her skin.

Despite what her mind was telling her, a strange paralysis left her immobile as his head came down slowly—infinitely slowly—and his warm, firm lips touched hers, lightly at first, testingly, then parting, applying more pressure, deepening until her lips, of their own accord, responded, softening under his. His body was tantalisingly close, though still not touching hers, his lips and the hand on her chin the only contact between them.

Then incredibly his mouth was no longer there. She saw his head draw back, felt his hand slide from her chin.

'I'd better go... Sleep tight, Caroline!' He almost growled the words as he turned on his heel and strode out.

She pushed the door closed behind him, leaning against it for support, breathing rapidly, shaking in every fibre of her being, as if he had swept her passionately into his arms instead of chastely brushing her lips with his.

That chaste kiss had had more of an impact than the most passionate kiss she had ever known!

She stumbled across the room, kicking off her shoes on the way, conscious of a hot clamminess from her damp palms to her burning cheeks. Halting in front of the oval mirror on the wall, she stared at the wide-eyed stranger in the glass. She saw a bewildered yearning in the uptilted grey eyes, a vulnerability about the soft lips that drew a groan from her. Had Armand Broch seen them too? Why was he having this effect on her? This man she despised, this man who had so cruelly hurt her own sister. 'Can't you trust me?' he'd said. Dear God, she'd rather trust a rattlesnake!

She flopped down on her bed, berating herself for her stupidity, her weakness. Hadn't she learnt anything from her sister's painful experience? Armand Broch was a dangerous man. He knew how dangerously attractive he was, and he traded on that knowledge. He had been merely playing with her tonight, amusing himself... perhaps feeling her out with a view to adding her to his score of conquests, only he had thought better of it at the last minute. Either he had decided that she wasn't worth the effort, or he had remembered who she was—the journalist who had come to do a write-up on him—and he didn't want to risk her exposing him as the womaniser he was!

Hysterical laughter rose in her throat. Oh, wasn't it the ultimate irony...Calli Smith going weak at the knees for the man who had broken her sister's heart? And she hadn't even put up a fight! *Knowing* the kind of man he was, she hadn't even put up a fight. That was the most galling part.

She dragged herself from the bed and wriggled out of her skirt and blouse, letting them lie where they fell.

Calli, you're a gullible little fool... She groaned as it all became clear to her. Can't you see he's just been trying to soften you up so that you won't ask him any difficult questions about his woman, about Stephanie? Can't you see that he's been cleverly eluding any personal questions all day? That preoccupied air of his at lunchtime and on the drive back to Château Broch... And tonight, pretending to be so weary, so in need of a relaxing drink! Men like Armand Broch don't get tired—ever!

Even that thoughtful gesture of his... offering you breakfast in bed. Can't you see he just wants a chance to go and see Davina—alone?

It was all so clear now—now that he was no longer casting his silken spell over her. If she hadn't been overtired, and a bit overwrought, she would never have reacted in that ridiculous way she had.

Best to forget it had ever happened. And to make sure it never happened again!

CHAPTER SIX

IT WAS another glorious autumn morning, and Armand had a smile on his lips when he picked Calli up at nine-thirty, after his early-morning visit to see Davina.

'The fine weather's still holding,' he enthused. 'It's great for the vintage. Only hope it lasts another couple of days.'

There was a marked softness in his eyes this morning, but Calli wasn't fooled by it. It would be Davina who had put it there, not Calli Smith.

'You saw Davina?' she asked coolly.

He nodded, but didn't elaborate. She hadn't expected him to.

It was another packed, long-drawn-out day. How Armand kept up this relentless pace, day after day, defeated Calli. He breezed through the day's engagements with his usual flair and energy. They spent part of the morning with Bill and Yvonne at the hospital, only leaving when Kurt arrived, repentant that he had been away from home when the accident had happened. Calli waited outside the intensive-care ward, and took a quick snap of the three as they emerged, happy with Bill's progress, though he would be in hospital for some time yet.

Armand's appointment with his tailor afterwards left his advertising team well-pleased with the result, and later, over lunch, Armand addressed a top football club on the subject of motivation, an impressive performance which, despite her private thoughts about him, stirred Calli as much as the rapt footballers. Later in the afternoon they visited his stables, just out of town, where she couldn't help being touched by Armand's caring attitude, his genuine love for his horses, their welfare seeming every bit as important to him as the commercial aspects which must have prompted his interest in the first place.

In all, she was quietly impressed by Armand's comments and his manner wherever he went, and she had to keep a tight rein on her emotions to maintain her loathing for him, reminding herself sternly that he was taking care to show her only his safe, businesslike side, and keeping his less attractive side, the side Stephanie knew all about, well hidden. Other than that uncommunicative nod earlier, he hadn't mentioned Davina or any of his other women all day. He certainly hadn't mentioned Stephanie or Roxy Manning! And that was the side of him she had to uncover, the side of him she must never overlook.

They were all at home for dinner that evening—Armand, his sister Leila, and Leila's husband Hamish, with Agnes bustling to and fro between the kitchen and the dining-room.

'How are you getting on with Davina?' Hamish asked at one point, and Calli's ears bristled.

'Not much progress,' Armand growled. 'But I'm still hopeful.' He caught Calli's eye and barked, 'I don't want any mention of Davina—you understand? At least, not until I give you the go-ahead.'

Not until Davina said yes? Calli shot him a direct look. But what was the woman supposed to be saying yes *to*? To marriage? An affair? Hardly marriage, Calli thought sourly. Not unless he is in the habit of using marriage as a lure, the way he had with Stephanie.

She realised he was still looking at her, and composed her features hurriedly. And after a moment his hard stare swivelled away, and he started asking Leila about the day's activities at the winery.

After dinner Leila confessed that she was just about ready to drop, and said she was going to bed to read for a while. Hamish said he had some work to do. As they both disappeared Armand told Calli he wanted to go through his mail and do some work in his office.

'Do you mind if I come too and take a photograph of you at your desk?' Calli asked, and he shrugged resignedly.

Shortly afterwards, as she was positioning herself to take a shot of him sitting at his desk, he asked lazily, 'Do you often take assignments away from home, Caroline?'

Her heart jumped. Was this the start of an interrogation? 'They come up fairly often,' she said cautiously. 'Maybe it's because I take good photographs as well as writing reasonable copy.'

'Your boyfriend doesn't mind you going away?'

'My boyfriend?'

'You're not telling me you don't *have* a boyfriend?'

'Not...really.' Why did he want to know? Did he want to start moving in on her himself? Her skin prickled. Don't be daft, Calli. He's not going to try anything...not here...and not with a camera pointing at him and a notebook in your hand.

'You're not *sure*?' Now there was a teasing light in his eye.

'There is someone I go out with...occasionally,' she admitted. So far she had resisted going steady with Andrew. He was nice, but——

'Just occasionally? Sounds a pretty wishy-washy relationship to me. Can't be much chemistry involved.'

'There's more to a relationship than just chemistry.' When she heard the sharpness in her tone she flushed. It wasn't just Armand and her own self-preservation she was thinking of. Armand sounded like Simon, her previous boyfriend. She had fallen rather hard for Simon—until it had dawned on her that all he had wanted was her body. Nothing else about her had interested him. It had been a disillusioning experience. She wanted more from a partner than cuddles and kisses. Simon had wanted more too... only what *he* had wanted she hadn't been prepared to give! Exit Simon.

'Oh, I agree,' Armand concurred easily. 'But it doesn't sound as if you're getting it from... what did you say his name was?'

'I didn't. Look, I'm the one who's supposed to be asking the questions. What about you, Armand?' She seized the opening he'd presented. 'Do *you* have a special relationship at the moment?' Tell me about Davina, she willed silently. Tell me about your other *special* relationships... if you dare.

'All my relationships are...special,' Armand said, his tone bantering. He had no intention of being pinned down. Obviously!

'Including your relationship with... Davina?' she hazarded.

His eyes flickered, a mocking glint in the green depths. 'Oh, yes... that's extremely special. *She's* special.'

'In what way?'

'In every way.' He leant back in his chair, his lips curving into a maddening smile. 'Are you taking a photograph or not?'

'You mean with that silly grin on your face?' As she raised her camera he laughed outright and held up his hand to stop her.

'OK, OK, don't waste your film. Wait till I start working. Is question time over?'

Wanting to wipe that infuriating smile from his face, she asked bluntly, 'What about your relationship with your secretary... Lauren, wasn't it? Is that special too?'

'But of course,' he said, his eyes still glimmering with amusement. Then abruptly his brow lowered and the bantering light faded from his eyes.

'I trust you're not jumping to all the wrong conclusions, Caroline... journalists have a habit of doing that. And you *are* a journalist. I tend to forget at times.'

'I won't go jumping to conclusions, I assure you,' she promised coolly. 'I told you my article will be... dead accurate. Anything I write will be based on pure fact.'

He frowned, as if not entirely reassured. Well might you worry, Calli thought with a flare of triumph. If you won't open up to me, Armand Broch, maybe someone else around here will!

'Might I remind you, Caroline... your article is supposed to be a week in my life. Not speculation about my relationships.' His tone was cool.

She drew in a deep breath. 'The readers will be interested in the kind of man you are, not just in what you do. But I promise I won't include any unfounded speculation. I told you, I deal in facts.'

'Just write about me as you see me.' His jaw tilted arrogantly.

'Oh, I will,' she said sweetly. He was so sure of himself! What a pleasure it would be to bring him down a notch or two! If he only knew what *she* knew about him he wouldn't look so smug! 'May I quote this conversation?' she asked.

He heaved a sigh. 'I'm sure you'll quote whatever you feel like quoting. Most journalists do, regardless of their protestations to the contrary.'

His cynical tone brought a swift denial from Calli. 'I'm not like that,' she assured him. 'If I promise something I will stick to it. You asked me earlier not to mention Davina—at least not yet. And so I won't. But may I ask if you expect a—a development in the next few days?'

'You mean while you are still here?' Amusement glimmered in his eyes. 'Possibly. I promise that, if there is, you will be the first to know.'

Calli bit her lip. She mistrusted that devilish look in his eye. Was he playing games with her, deliberately throwing out hints of a possible scoop, simply to get a reaction? Or was he merely afraid that by speaking up too soon he might end up with egg on his face if Davina rejected him outright?

She sighed, and shook her head. 'No wonder there are so many rumours spread about you,' she said in exasperation. 'I see now how they start. You start them yourself, by tossing around vague hints and being provocative and mysterious.'

'Do I?' He looked surprised. 'It must be a reflex action when I'm around journalists. Look, shall we stop and start again? We want this article to be dead accurate, to use your own words.' He smiled disarmingly, and involuntarily she found her own lips twitching in response. Charming devil, she thought, and deliberately conjured up Stephanie's agonised face so that she could arm herself against the potent charm of this man.

'I promise I'll watch what I say in future,' he added solemnly.

'I'd rather you be open and honest.' Some hope, she thought, with your record.

'Well, I'll try. Fire away,' he invited silkily.

Hoping to catch him off-guard, Calli asked promptly, 'Is it true that you were romantically involved with...Stephanie Fox while she was here?' She mouthed her sister's name with difficulty, concentrating on keeping her expression bland.

Armand's face hardened. 'Where did you hear that?' he rasped.

She swallowed. 'Word gets around... You're both in the public spotlight. It must have been...the gossip columns...I don't recall.'

His brow shot up. 'You should never believe what you read in the gossip columns, Caroline. A man can't be seen with a woman without those sharks jumping to conclusions. *Romantically* involved!' He gave a snort. His tone was scathing—an insult to her sister. 'You can quote me on *this*, Caroline Barr Smith...I was never *seriously* involved with Stephanie Fox. Matter closed.' His eyes told her he meant it.

He was admitting an involvement, but denying that it was ever serious. Outraged, but determined to hide it, Calli moved swiftly past him to the window. 'Do you mind if I draw the curtains?' she asked in a muffled voice. 'It'll make a better backdrop for my next shot.' It was no use asking Armand Broch any personal questions. No use at all! He would never open up to her—to a mere journalist! Let alone tell the truth.

As she was turning back to retrieve her camera she noticed Armand pluck a key from a compartment in his desk and unlock one of the drawers underneath. She caught her breath as he drew out a leather-bound diary and set it down unopened in front of him. His appointment book? Or...his personal diary? What she wouldn't give to take a peek inside, if it were the latter!

She felt a rush of heat to her cheeks. Not that she would dream of using anything he'd written, even if she had a chance to read it. It wouldn't be ethical.

A bitter voice whispered in her ear, Was he ethical in his treatment of your sister? What was ethical about pretending to love a woman, actually proposing marriage, and then cold-bloodedly making love to another woman while both were still guests in his home? Armand had broken her sister's heart and threatened her career, and he couldn't have cared less, the bastard.

What if it was all in his diary...all the sordid details, and maybe even details of other women he had hurt and betrayed in the same way? She'd be crazy not to seize the chance to get her hands on such dynamite! The general public saw Armand Broch as a harmless Don Juan, a good-looking bachelor simply having a good time, simply taking what was on offer. They knew nothing about the lies he told, the two-timing, the heartbreak he left in his wake. Calli owed it to her sister—and other women—to reveal the heartless monster that lay behind the devil-may-care façade.

She plotted how she could do it as she changed the film in her camera and took a last shot of Armand at his desk, surreptitiously dropping the finished film on to the carpet and kicking it under her chair while Armand wasn't looking.

She wouldn't, of course, be silly enough to steal the diary, or even refer to its existence in her article. Just thumbing through it—seeing written proof, in Armand's own hand—would be enough to give her the courage to

write the truth about him. She would make no mention
of Stephanie—not by name—or any of his other women
either. They were just pawns, innocent victims. It was
Armand Broch she wanted to expose. And he deserved
everything that was coming to him!

She was half asleep when she heard a door bang. Armand
must have decided at last to go to bed. Her heart began
to beat like a tom-tom, and she wondered if she dared
do it.

She knew that if she thought about it she never would.

Hauling herself out of the warmth, she slipped on her
robe and slippers and tiptoed to the door, quietly opening
it and peeping out. There wasn't a sound. Moonlight
shone in through the overhead windows of the deserted
gallery, lighting her way as she crept towards Armand's
office, guiltily aware of the disapproving eyes staring
down from the portraits lining the walls.

Tentatively she opened the office door. The room was
in darkness. With the drapes still drawn there was no
moonlight to guide her. She fumbled her way to the desk,
felt for the lamp, and switched it on.

There was no sign of Armand's diary on his desk. Not
that she had expected him to leave it there for prying
eyes. But she knew where he kept it. Locked in one of
the drawers. And she knew that he kept the key to the
drawer in one of the tiny compartments above, because
she had watched him take it out. All she had to do was
retrieve the key and . . .

She leaned on the desk for a second, her breath coming
in ragged gasps. She had never done anything like this
before—sneaking around, spying on people. It was only
the thought of Stephanie's suffering that had brought
her this far.

She thrust out her hand and tugged the tiny compartment open. She saw the tiny key lying inside. And then the enormity of what she was doing hit her, and she snapped it shut again. She couldn't do it. What in the world had possessed her to believe that she could? No matter what revelations Armand had entrusted to the pages of his diary, they were private, and she would be betraying his trust and her own integrity if she attempted to read them.

She stood for a moment clutching her chest and gulping deep breaths of air, appalled at what she had almost done. Armand might have wronged her sister and a dozen other women, but two wrongs didn't make a right. She would have to find some other way to expose him . . . a more honest, open way. Or she would never be able to live with herself!

She straightened, and backed away from the desk, and at that precise moment she heard the click of the door behind her, and swung round with a stifled gasp to see Armand halt in the doorway, the angle of the desk lamp throwing his face into sinister shadow.

'Caroline! What are you doing in here?' He was clutching a book, Calli noticed. He must have gone into the library opposite to fetch something to read and noticed the light come on in his office.

'I . . . I——' She staggered back against the desk as he crossed the room in one long stride and stood over her, his stance vaguely menacing.

'Looking for something?' His eyes were flat, hard, and she felt a strange little tug inside. He was looking at her with such . . . cold suspicion. And perhaps disappointment too. And she couldn't blame him! She threw up a little prayer of thanks that she had changed her mind about the diary. And that she had come prepared.

'Yes, I—I came to look for that film, Armand. The one I took out of my camera earlier.' She tried to speak calmly, not to gabble, not to sound as guilty as she felt. 'I—I think I must have left it in here somewhere...'

'Couldn't it have waited until morning?' She was relieved when his eyes flicked away from her face to sweep round the room. 'I can't see any film,' he said coldly. He didn't believe her, obviously.

'It has to be here somewhere...' She moved across to the chair where she had been sitting earlier in the evening, and prodded around for a moment. Then she dropped to her knees and felt underneath. 'Ah!' Her fingers closed over the film she had had the foresight earlier to kick under the chair. She held it up triumphantly. 'Here it is!' She smiled brightly, hoping her cheeks weren't as flushed as they felt.

At the same time she became aware of her flimsy attire, of her robe gaping open at the front, revealing the deep shadow between her pale breasts. She fumbled ineffectually with her fingers to close the gap, hoping he would put her flushed cheeks down to embarrassment. 'I—I'm sorry if I disturbed you,' she gasped, inching towards the door. 'Goodnight, Armand!'

She felt his eyes following her as she fled the room. His lips were pursed, his eyes thoughtful, still cool. Had she convinced him that it was the film which had brought her back here, and not...? Oh, dear lord, don't let him guess the real reason, she panicked as she scurried back to her room. Much as she despised Armand Broch for what he had done to her sister, much as he deserved to be spied on and exposed, she didn't want him thinking that she would stoop to that low level... especially since she had decided she couldn't go through with it!

She wasn't sure why his good opinion was so important to her. Was it because she was afraid of being sent away before she had completed her assignment? Or could there be a more...? No, that was ridiculous! Why should she care what Armand Broch thought of her? She *didn't* care!

When she came down for breakfast it was to find that Armand had already had his and had gone out to inspect the winery operations. Without waiting for her!

Her heart sank. Was that an ominous sign?

She gulped down her breakfast, grabbed her notebook and camera, and flew outside, almost colliding with Armand as he emerged from one of the cellars.

Relief flew through her when he halted and smiled down at her. Surely he wouldn't be smiling like that if he believed...?

She shook herself and smiled back, her relief bringing a new brightness to her dark-fringed grey eyes.

'Do you mind if I follow you around?' she asked breathlessly.

'Do I have any choice?' There was more amused tolerance than coolness in his tone, she was glad to hear. 'I've just been checking how things are going before I start work for the day. Come with me while I take a wander through the vineyard and have a chat with the pickers. I like to get to know them, and for them to get to know me.'

As they emerged from the shadows and headed off together Calli found herself blinking against the harsh glare of the morning sun, already packing a decided punch. It was going to be a sweltering hot day—unusual for this time of year. Maybe that was why Armand was in such a good mood.

He seemed to confirm it when he said, glancing up at the sky, 'We're having a real Indian summer, aren't we? It's going to be a bumper vintage.' His green eyes were glowing in a way that made her want to enthuse along with him. Instead, as he raised a hand to shield his eyes against the glare, she lifted her camera and took a shot of him. No matter what she thought of him as a person, as a man he was heart-stoppingly attractive—the raw-boned arrogance of his profile, the sinewy line of his long body, the athletic grace of his stance making him a perfect subject for a photographer. As for her feelings as a woman, she was making sure she kept those firmly under wraps.

'The pickers start work at seven-thirty each morning and finish at four,' Armand informed her as they strolled past the beds of roses, drinking in the sweet heavy scent. 'The locals go home each day, and the rest stay at the local caravan park or with friends. They keep fairly much to themselves. They bring a cut lunch and eat it in the shade of the gums and peppercorn trees.'

Calli nodded, storing away everything he said for possible use later in her article, just as she would eventually sift through all the photographs she took of him to pick out the best ones to use.

The vines on the slopes stretched away in leafy rows, brilliantly green beneath the soft blue sky and the bright sun, the yellow tips on the vines glinting like gold. Armand strode on ahead, pausing when he came to a woman picker in a red hat. Calli followed more leisurely, her tension easing bit by bit as the sun's warmth seeped into her bones and the scent of the ripe grapes filled her nostrils. She took a shot of Armand with the woman, noting that the picker's skin was dry and reddened, her hands calloused from deftly snipping the ripened bunches of grapes from the vines. The woman was looking at Armand with animation and ... with respect, Calli had to admit. All the people who worked for him, she mused, appeared to respect him. Because he showed an interest in them, she guessed. Not many big bosses would take the time, or care. One had to admire him for that, no matter what one thought of him in ... other ways.

As Armand moved on she followed, drinking in the warmth and the beauty of her surroundings. She saw a movement on the other side of the trellis of vines, beyond the curtain of green. Only hands were visible, picking busily. A peal of laughter rose from the vines. Other laughter followed, deep and rumbling. For a moment a sense of timelessness came over her, spreading over her like a soothing blanket. She paused, sighing, aware of a strange contentment. A girl could come to love this place.

'Caroline, come and look at this ...' Armand's rich voice rang out, and she felt a tiny flutter inside—only to bite her lip guiltily. She mustn't let her heart flutter for Armand Broch. She must never forget that he was the man who had callously betrayed her own sister, making promises he had never intended to keep.

She came back to cold reality, and with a stifled sigh hastened to join him, her face set in an impassive mask.

CHAPTER SEVEN

CALLI met Armand's secretary Lauren for the first time later in the morning in Armand's office, and again over a casual lunch on the leafy terrace at the rear of the château with Leila and Hamish and other members of the office staff. Lauren was a tall, athletic redhead with a ready smile and dancing blue eyes. She and Armand had an easy rapport which made Calli wonder again if their relationship was closer than boss and secretary... or had been in the past.

'Caroline, I'm expecting a visitor shortly from the Wine Research Institute,' Armand said as everyone dispersed after the meal and went back to work. 'I'll be meeting him in my office, and our discussion will be confidential. Mention the meeting in your article, by all means, but I'd prefer it if you left us alone while he's here.'

'Of course.'

'Anyway, it will give you a chance to put your feet up and read a book or write a letter or whatever you like to do in your spare time.' There was a look in his eyes that gave her the feeling that he had forgiven her for stealing into his office last night, and, just as he had pleaded with her the other night to trust him, now she found she wanted to show him that he could rely on her.

'Armand, would you let me help Leila in the tasting-room? She looked so tired at lunchtime—she barely ate a thing, and she rushed off again after only a few minutes because there were more busloads of tourists arriving.

96

Maybe if I could help her out for a while...' She looked up at him questioningly.

For a fleeting second she saw a glimmer of doubt in his eyes, as if he suspected it might be a ploy on her part to grill Leila about him while he was safely out of the way. Nothing, she realised in dismay, had been further from her mind. She would never intrude on Leila's busiest hours, especially when she was plainly under stress. She tried to tell Armand that with her eyes, gazing unblinkingly up at him.

'I'm sure she'd appreciate it,' he said finally, his expression changing, seeming to soften, as his eyes searched hers. 'I'll join you after my visitor has gone.'

Leila did appreciate her offer of help, almost hugging her with relief, and Calli became so immersed in the tasks Leila had set her that she didn't realise how much time had passed until she came face to face with Armand as she was rushing to clear one of the tables.

'Armand, I didn't see you!' she gulped as he caught her arm, sending shivery tingles along her bare skin. 'H-how long have you been waiting for me?'

'I haven't been waiting for you—I've been watching you,' he admitted. 'I think I'll offer you a job!'

She felt herself blushing. 'I've enjoyed it. The last busload is almost ready to leave. Shall I go on or...come with you?'

'I'll stay and lend a hand too. There's nothing too pressing in the office. Lauren knows where I am if anything comes up.'

He was as good as his word, and it wasn't until the last bus had driven away and the tasting-room had closed down for the day that either of them paused for breath, other than one brief moment when Calli retrieved her camera from where she had left it and took a shot of

Armand packing a crate of wine bottles for a buyer. Until then she had almost forgotten her real reason for coming to Château Broch!

She had a rueful smile on her lips as the two of them strolled back to the château together. A week in Armand Broch's life was turning out to be a real eye-opener. 'How do you keep it up, week after week?' she heard herself asking. 'You never seem to stop.'

He shrugged as he answered, 'It's always hectic at vintage time. It's our busiest time of year.'

She eyed him thoughtfully. Even at normal times she couldn't imagine him slackening his pace. He had so many responsibilities, so many interests and concerns, as well as the unexpected incidents which kept cropping up. 'And what about all the interstate and overseas travelling you must do at other times?' she asked. 'That must take up a lot of your time as well.'

He didn't deny it. 'I like to keep busy. I enjoy it.'

He did seem to thrive on it, she had to admit. She had never known anyone with so much coiled-up energy inside. And yet, for all his busy schedule, he had managed to find the time this week to take charge of two injured employees—one not even his, but his brother Kurt's—and to lend a hand this afternoon in the tasting-room, just like any other member of his staff. No wonder his staff thought so highly of him. Leila was certainly grateful—she had been warm in her praise for both of them, and already she was looking less stressed than she had at lunchtime.

'Is that why you haven't married?' she asked boldly. 'Because you're always on the move? Because it would tie you down too much? Because you're afraid your hectic lifestyle wouldn't be fair on a wife, that she might end up feeling neglected?'

Her barrage of questions brought a faint smile to his lips. 'Wrong on all counts. If I had a wife I would see that she didn't feel neglected,' he said flatly. 'I told you before—I haven't married because up until now I haven't met a woman I would want to share my life with.'

Had he forgotten Stephanie already? Calli wondered with a swift shaft of pain. 'But you're happy to share your bed.' As the accusation popped out she drew in a sharp breath. But she didn't retract it, valiantly meeting him eye to eye—and waiting for the explosion. It didn't come.

'Sure...why not? I haven't exactly lacked willing partners. And each one has known the score...I've never pretended it would lead to anything long-term.'

She tried to suppress the fury that rose in her throat. '*None* of them has expected any more of you?' She forced the question out. What about Stephanie? she wanted to shout at him.

'Some of them might have *hoped* for more, but I've never led a woman on, I've never promised what I didn't intend to deliver.'

Lying, arrogant bastard! she fumed silently. She forced out another question, determined to pin him down. 'You've never proposed marriage...and then had second thoughts?' Could that have been what had happened with Stephanie? Was it possible that Armand, perhaps swept away by passion one night, had proposed to her sister in good faith, thinking in that moment that they could make it work...only to realise later that it never could, with Stephanie's career and his own workload dooming it to failure?

But that wouldn't excuse what he had done so soon afterwards...taking Roxy Manning into his bed, without first breaking off his relationship with Stephanie. Unless he had *tried* to break it off, and Stephanie, besotted as she was, wouldn't let him go!

'Now why would you ask a question like that?' She realised that Armand was watching her with an odd expression, his face tightening, and she swallowed, and said quickly,

'Just...checking. Trying to get the facts.'

'Ah, yes, the facts. We want them to be dead accurate, don't we? Well, take this aboard, my assiduous young newshound: I have never had second thoughts about a proposal because I have never proposed—incredible though that may seem to you and the world in general. I've never even been close to it. Got that?'

'Got it,' she said in a muffled voice, looking away in confusion. He sounded so...adamant, so...genuine. And yet—he had to be lying! Of course he was. He had no idea, of course, that she had heard the truth from her own sister, that she had seen her sister's suffering with her own eyes. And Stephanie's tears, her distress, had been very real. Fine actress though she was, her anguish had been no act.

No...Armand was lying. He had to be. Why else would he refuse to talk about Stephanie? Why else would his family avoid talking about her? Much as Calli wanted to trust Armand, to believe him, how could she? She gave a tremulous sigh. Maybe, if she made more of an effort, she could persuade Armand's brother-in-law Hamish to open up about Stephanie and Armand. She had to find out the truth. She had to!

Because the evening was so warm the family had dinner alfresco-style on the leafy terrace where they had had lunch, and as usual the vintage was the main topic of conversation. No mention was made of Davina, or of the movie which had been filmed on their doorstep—and certainly no mention was made of Stephanie—and Calli guessed it was because Armand was present. If Armand had nothing to hide, why were they being so reticent, so protective?

'Have you got a minute?' Armand asked Leila after dinner. 'I'd like to discuss a few things with you ... to do with our wine sales.'

'Sure.'

'I'll be in the lab,' said Hamish, and, with a cheery wave, ambled off. Calli's eyes followed him. Was this her chance to speak to him alone?

'Mind if I go for a stroll in the fresh air?' she asked Armand carelessly.

Armand gave her a quick look, before he shrugged and said, 'Why not? You deserve a break.' Was he implying that he needed a break too? Calli wondered ruefully as she left them. Not that she could blame him for wanting her out of the way when he had his private talk with Leila. The man had to have some privacy! Maybe afterwards he would grab the chance to jump into his car and race off to town to meet Davina. With his leech of a journalist out of the way, he could let his hair down and stay the night with her if he wanted to.

She shut her mind to the thought. She had other things to do and think about, while she had the chance.

She made her way in the sultry darkness to the building which housed Hamish's laboratory.

'Hello.' Hamish looked up, blinking in surprise as she poked her head in the door—her cheeks flaming suddenly as she remembered how even Armand had knocked before entering Hamish's domain.

'I'm sorry—am I allowed to come in?' she asked tentatively, her gaze flicking round the clinical white-walled room with its tightly stacked shelves and cluttered bench-tops.

'Er—sure. What brings you here, Caroline?' Leaving his bench, Hamish hastened over to join her. 'I can think of more interesting places for a young girl to spend her evenings than a dreary laboratory.'

'I really came to see you,' she admitted, stepping into the room as he waved her to a chair.

'Well...it's not often pretty ladies come to visit old Hamish in his lair.' Hamish looked faintly discomfited, she thought. Was he uneasy about what she was going to ask him?

'What do you mean, *old*?' she laughed. He couldn't be much older than Armand, though his hair was already thinning on top. 'And I can't believe that pretty ladies have never come to visit you. Didn't Stephanie Fox ever come to your lab while she was here?' she asked teasingly, grabbing the opening he'd presented her.

'Stephanie Fox? What makes you think that a beautiful movie star would be interested in my dreary laboratory?' His lip quirked as he spoke, but there was a wary inflexion in his voice that warned her she must tread carefully if she wanted to draw him out about Armand's affair with Stephanie. Hamish was Armand Broch's brother-in-law—and a trusted colleague. His loyalty would be to Armand, not to Stephanie, no matter how badly he thought Armand might have treated her.

'Well, I understood she and Armand were...close for a time,' she ventured. 'And as you are Armand's brother-in-law...' She paused, hoping he would take it from there. When he didn't she asked innocently, 'What did you think of her?'

'I thought she was a stunner,' Hamish said frankly. 'Those eyes! No wonder——' He stopped.

'No wonder Armand fell for her?' Calli prompted.

He shrugged. 'Well...no one was surprised when they——' He stopped, and took a deep breath. 'Look, there was nothing to it. Nothing lasting, I mean. It was just...' His voice trailed off again as he glanced towards the door. And then she heard it too. Heavy footsteps, coming this way. Oh, no, she thought, not Armand!

'I'd better not hold you up any longer.' She rose hastily to her feet. Would Hamish tell Armand that she had been asking questions about him and Stephanie? Her eyes flew to Hamish's workbench, seeking a diversion, a different topic of conversation. Scattered corks lay on the shiny bench-top. She drifted closer, feigning an interest—and just then the door swung open.

'Caroline!' Armand halted in surprise. 'What do you think you're doing?' he rasped. He glanced at Hamish as he spoke, a faint frown creasing his brow, as if he guessed she had come here to quiz Hamish.

A wave of shame washed over her at the thought of coming here behind his back, even though he must know it was her job to piece together a rounded picture of him for her article. She stepped forward quickly, answering a trifle breathlessly, 'I—I didn't think you would mind if I popped in for a moment to say hello. Hamish has been very kind, but I—I was just leaving.'

Armand nodded curtly. Dismissively. 'I want a word with Hamish. You run along.' His tone was sharp.

Cheeks burning, she ran—hoping he wouldn't question Hamish, hoping Hamish wouldn't tell him that she had been asking questions about Stephanie, causing Armand to wonder *why* she was so interested in his relationship with the actress, and perhaps to guess that her interest wasn't solely professional. If he was to guess who she was...

Damn, damn, damn! Why had she rushed in and bombarded Hamish with questions about Stephanie? Why couldn't she have spent more time building up his trust first—his and Leila's—and waited for them to open up of their own accord?

But would they have ever opened up without some prompting from her? She only had a week, and time was fast running out!

And now Armand would trust her less than ever! The thought caused a pang that made her grip her hands in confusion. Why should she care what Armand Broch thought of her? Because now he would clam up even further? Or…was there something more personal behind it? She made a muffled sound, half angry, half bewildered.

A full moon was rising as she headed back to the château. A faint breeze stirred the dry leaves in her path, and from somewhere high in the branches came the eerie hoot of an owl.

She sighed, feeling suddenly restless and dispirited. She didn't want to go up to her room just yet; she certainly didn't want to go to bed. She knew she would just lie there thinking about Armand Broch, and about Stephanie, and about her own foolish, mixed-up feelings. It had hurt to hear that sharp, cool note in Armand's voice just now, and to know it was because he suspected her of asking questions about a subject he had warned her was taboo. It hurt her even more to know that she had given him cause to be suspicious.

Almost of their own volition, her footsteps veered to the right, and she found herself heading for the rows of vines. A stroll in the moonlight might calm her mind and help her to sleep.

The pungent smell of ripe grapes rose from the vines. Other scents—earthy, leafy scents—drifted in the air. The lush vines stretched away in misty rows, veiled in a shimmer of light. To the west, the tall poplars were black against the pale, light-drenched sky.

She kept walking until she reached the man-made lagoon. The evening was deliciously warm; one of those balmy autumn nights that the valley people tended to accept without much fuss, seeing it only in terms of how it would 'improve the vintage', but which to Calli was rare and beautiful, a time to be savoured.

The surface of the lagoon was like milky glass in the moonlight. The water looked irresistibly inviting. Calli kicked off her sandals and dipped her toes in. The water was pleasantly warm, not at all cold. An overwhelming urge seized her to throw off her clothes and take a swim in the pearly water, to feel it flowing sensuously, relaxingly over her body, cooling her flushed skin and washing away her tension.

On an impulse she peeled off her skirt and blouse, and, with a quick glance round, stripped down to her bare skin. Lowering her slim white body into the water, she stretched full-length, her fingers just touching the pebbly bottom. She felt the moonlight flooding down from the sky, the water stroking her flanks as she moved along slowly, silently, keeping close to the bank.

'Nice evening for a dip.'

Her eyes leapt round in dismay, her head nearly jerking from her shoulders. She could happily have died! A tall figure stood at the edge of the lagoon, hands on hips, lips parted, teeth gleaming in the moonlight. Armand! Armand Broch, of all people!

'G-go away!' she gasped, aware that her nakedness must be clearly visible to him. 'I—I thought there was no one around... H-how long have you been there?'

He merely laughed, unmoved and unmoving.

'Armand!' she said warningly, trying to sound threatening, and failing miserably.

'Agnes told me you hadn't come back to the house,' he said chattily, taking, if anything, a step closer. 'I came looking for you.'

'P-please, Armand. I want to get out.'

'May I fetch your towel? Or didn't you bring one?'

'No! I mean—oh, just *go*, Armand, *please*! She was starting to feel cold now, tiny goose-bumps breaking out on her skin. But her face felt flaming hot. He must think her an absolute wanton! How did Armand Broch deal with wanton women? she wondered uneasily.

Alarmed, she huddled in the water, her arms clasped across her naked breasts.

'Armand, I never would have——' She broke off, biting her lip. She was only making things worse. She started again, more forcefully, though her teeth were chattering like castanets, as much from nervous reaction as from the cold. 'The water looked so inviting that I j-jumped in without thinking.' She sighed at her lame defence. She was making it sound as if she often acted foolishly without thinking!

'Here.' He peeled off his shirt and threw it down within her reach. 'Mop yourself up with that and then get dressed. I'll turn my back.'

'Th-thank you,' she stammered. 'B-but I'd rather you w-went.'

'And what if someone else comes along? They might not be so broad-minded. Or such a... gentleman.' The sardonic way he uttered the word 'gentleman' made it sound dangerously as if he meant precisely the opposite. 'I'll keep a watchful eye out for you,' he offered generously. 'Are you out yet?'

'No, I'm not! Don't look round!' She was reaching out for the shirt on the bank, watching him warily as she eased herself out of the water. Wrapping the shirt loosely around her, she darted to her pile of clothes, scooped them up and dived for the shelter of the vines.

Dabbing her dripping body frantically with Armand's white shirt, she wriggled her feet into her sandals, debating rather hysterically whether to burst into helpless giggles—or to run for her life. Instead, with fumbling fingers and a galloping heart, she struggled into her panties and bra.

'Dressed yet?' came a playful voice from behind the vines.

'N-nearly. Not yet!'

She pulled on her skirt and snatched up her blouse. Her fingers were shaking so much that she had difficulty managing the buttons.

'Can I help?'

She caught her breath, her head snapping round, her legs threatening to crumple beneath her. He was standing only an arm's length away, the smooth outline of his muscular chest, bare to the waist, silhouetted against the pale sky. The devil! He hadn't waited...

She couldn't think any further than that, couldn't trust herself to remonstrate aloud. She made a pathetic attempt to finish the task she was doing, only to feel a warm hand close over her trembling fingers.

'You're cold. Let me do it.'

Her hand froze under his touch. She was powerless to resist, powerless to pull away, even when, instead of fastening her buttons, he slipped his hand inside the front of her blouse and trailed light fingertips over the swell of her breast. Her heart thudded beneath his fingers, her breathing quickening, her cool skin turning instantly to fire.

'Your skin is so soft, Caroline...so smooth,' he said huskily. 'And your body...it's exquisite...as white as the moon.'

She stiffened in his arms. 'You did see me!' she croaked, but she didn't pull away; she couldn't. The touch of his hand on her fiery skin was paralysing her.

'Did I? Does it matter?' His fingers continued to gently massage the soft curves beneath the unbuttoned blouse, while his other hand slid up her back, his fingers tracing the line of her shoulder-blade. 'Let me see you now, Caroline...as you were before. Don't be afraid. I won't hurt you, I promise...'

The word 'hurt' triggered an alarm bell in her brain. Aghast, she saw the deep slumbrous passion in his eyes; was giddily aware of the smooth width of his bare chest, inviting her caresses. What was she doing, languishing in the arms of the man who had hurt her sister? Poor Stephanie, who had foolishly loved him and trusted him, who must have seen that same look, felt those same hands on her body, heard those same words from his lips!

'Stop!'

She tried to wrench herself free, but the hand on her back restrained her, while the rhythmical motion of his fingers on her breast persisted.

'Armand, I mean it...let me go! *Please!*' The cry was torn from her.

His fingers finally stilled on her burning flesh. His eyes sought hers, smouldering like emerald fire in the moonlight. Slowly he withdrew his hand, a look of baffled whimsy replacing the desire in his eyes. The hand on her back dropped away, and without a word he began to rebutton her blouse.

It gave her a moment's respite to fight down the emotions that had been threatening to take control of her, weakening her so that she hadn't known what she was doing. Never again, she vowed weakly, would she be involved with anything that brought her this close to him again... anything that could threaten to fracture the tenuous hold she had on her emotions.

'Caroline...' He spoke at last, touching her cheek with a sensitive fingertip, almost drawing another cry from her lips. 'I'm sorry. I should have known... that you would be different, that you weren't being deliberately provocative. Forgive me?'

She nodded numbly, turning quickly away, not wanting him to read the emotions that must be reflected in her eyes. Forgive *him*? Oh, Stephanie, she cried silently, forgive *me*! I came here to do a job, to expose Armand Broch for what he did to you and to other women, not to fall weakly under the spell of the very man who hurt you and drove you away!

She began to walk away, mindlessly putting one leg in front of the other, hardly aware of the vines tugging at her arm, brushing her cheek.

'It was my fault,' she said stiltedly over her shoulder. 'I don't know what came over me.' He could take that any way he wished... as a reference to her dip in the lagoon—or to the way she had responded to his advances. Why, oh, why hadn't she pushed him away the second he'd touched her?

Armand caught up with her. He was dragging his discarded shirt in one hand, his bare chest gleaming in the moonlight. His voice, close to her ear, sent further shock waves through her.

'What came over you, Caroline, was an entirely natural reaction to a balmy South Australian evening. I was the one who over-reacted. I...' he seemed to be having difficulty finding the right words, a rare thing for the self-possessed head of Château Broch '... I have nothing but respect for you, Caroline, believe me. Not that I'm saying I want you to forget what happened— well, not entirely. You're a beautiful woman—a man would have to be made of stone not to be affected by the sight of...' He let the rest trail off as two huge grey eyes leapt to his in dismay. 'All I'm saying is, I wish I had been less... clumsy.'

'Let's forget it.' She gave a trembling sigh. Armand Broch had remembered in time who he was... the powerful head of the Château Broch Winery. And who *she* was... merely a journalist here on an assignment, who would soon be on her way.

'What a pity you didn't have your camera with you.' His tone was bantering now as he deliberately introduced a lighter note. 'What a scene that would have been for your article!'

Her cheeks flaming, her eyes flew to his. The amusement in his eyes almost fooled her for a second, until she remembered the kind of man he was, and wondered what lay behind that teasing remark of his. Her mistrust of him provided the answer. He was telling her that if she wrote about the advances he had made just now she would also have to admit that she had provoked them by going swimming in the nude. It's blackmail! she thought.

Anger warred for a moment with her own sense of humour, her sense of fun finally winning out, plucking a reluctant smile from her lips.

'Don't worry. This will be entirely off the record,' she promised him.

'I think that is very wise,' he agreed solemnly, and for a fleeting moment their eyes met in perfect accord.

Why had he come looking for her in the first place? she wondered now.

'You were looking for me, you said.' She injected an impassive, businesslike note into her voice to show him she was ready to forget what had happened.

'Well, yes, I was. I wanted to apologise. I'm afraid I was a bit abrupt with you earlier. In the lab. I had...something on my mind.'

Yes, she thought, her eyes narrowing in the silvery half-light. You were worried about what Hamish might have told me...

And now he wanted to apologise? Hamish couldn't have told any tales after all. Good old Hamish.

'Please—forget it,' she said again, quickening her steps. Armand must have a guilty conscience...or he wouldn't care what his brother-in-law might have told her.

'On our way back,' Armand said matter-of-factly, 'I want to fetch some wine from our private cellar. Like to come with me? You haven't seen the family cellar yet, have you?'

'No, I haven't. All right.' Was it an upswing in the breeze that caused a faint shiver to glide down the back of her neck? Or the thought of being alone again—in a confined space—with Armand Broch?

But there was nothing to fear...not any longer. The moment of madness was past...it was behind them.

Forgotten. More than that, *regretted*. Armand had said so. She had nothing to fear other than her own...

Stephanie's face rose in front of her, her lovely dark eyes swollen with tears, and her trembling lips seemed to be mouthing the words 'Beware, Calli...beware of this man'.

The vines on either side rustled in the breeze, as though whispering a warning. Calli stifled a sigh. Armand seemed so honourable in so many ways... How could he have treated Stephanie so shabbily, so...callously?

CHAPTER EIGHT

NEITHER spoke as they crossed the paved courtyard to the secluded north side of the château, the moonlight filtering through the trees on to the pale sandstone walls. The shuttered windows and heavy doors were cast into deep shadow.

'Here we are.' Armand pushed aside the trailing ivy and led the way down a flight of moss-covered steps. Producing a key from the pocket of his trousers, he thrust open the heavy oak door.

'Wait here... I'll go in first and turn on the lights.'

Calli shivered as she followed him, feeling rather as though she had been transported back into medieval times, when dungeons were dimly lit and crypts oddly foreboding. The thick stone archways and oppressively low ceiling, and the dark shadows playing on the weathered oaken casks and rows of neatly stacked bottles, with bare light-bulbs providing the only illumination, had a chilling effect.

Armand, having knotted his damp shirt loosely around his hips to free his hands, was lighting a candle, which he then set down on a cask with an intricately carved face, while he extracted two glasses from the shelf behind.

'Have a glass of port, Caroline, to warm you,' he invited, the rich rumble of his voice dispelling the gloomy atmosphere. He drew rich red wine from the cask in front of him and handed her a half-filled glass.

'It's a vintage tawny port,' he said, and grinned suddenly. 'Sounds contradictory, doesn't it? Tawny ports are usually blends of various years. This one is called a *vintage* tawny because it is made from one particular year. It's very rich. Try it.'

She sniffed it first, as she had seen the others doing.

'Mm. Smells good.' She sipped, swirling it round in her mouth, tasting its fullness, the rich tannin finish. She let it slide down her throat. 'Tastes good, too. Would you say...a full-flavoured wine with plenty of character?' she enquired archly.

'You're learning.' Armand raised his own glass and tested the nose of his own wine. 'It's an outstanding after-dinner wine, this. It'll go on maturing for years.'

The wine was warming her inside; relaxing her too. They sipped companionably until their glasses were empty.

'Now...follow me.' Picking up the candle to throw extra light in their path, Armand led her deeper into the cellar. Here there were only bottles, racks and racks of them, with barely room to walk between. At the end of one row Armand paused before an arched stone alcove filled with more bottles. He turned to her with a smile that made her stomach coil into a knot. It was a smile that even in the dim light had a softening effect, smoothing out the cynical lines of his face and giving the sardonic eyes a glittering warmth.

'I want to select some wines for tomorrow night.' His voice was startlingly resonant in the eerie silence. 'My brother Kurt and sister-in-law Amy and their two tomboy daughters are coming to stay overnight. You'll join us for dinner too, of course.'

He looked down at her, and she nodded, feeling suddenly shy—not nervous, *shy*—unable to trust her own voice. She was sharply aware of the damp earthiness rising from the floor, the musty smell of old bottles, the pressing stone walls. The silence lengthened and still he didn't move, his eyes imprisoning hers, the candle in his hand flickering between them. She stared back, incapable of looking away. There was something hypnotic about those steadfast green eyes.

She jumped when he spoke again.

'If you go on looking at me like that, Caroline, I'm not going to be able to leave you alone.'

She blinked, but still couldn't seem to break the spell; she was mesmerised—stunned—by the burning desire she saw in his eyes. Her body pulsed with a deep, aching response, a need so great that it was a tangible pain. She knew she had to fight it and, with her eyes still clinging to his, she attempted to back away, but the cold stone wall prevented her. She saw the flare of the candle dance away; realised that Armand was placing it on a ledge in the wall behind him. Nervously she flicked the tip of her tongue over her parted lips.

'Heavens, Caroline, what do you think I'm made of? How can I leave you alone when you look at me like that? Come here...'

It wasn't really an invitation—it wasn't even a command. Already he was pulling her into his arms, burying his warm lips in the soft curve of her throat. She gave a soft moan, which seemed to inflame him further. He ran his fingers through her hair while he slid his other arm across the lower part of her back, pressing her against him in a way that sent pulses of hot blood throbbing through her, deep, deep down. Slowly his lips moved upward, trailing hot kisses along her throat, her jawline, her cheek, in a blazing path to her lips.

She felt her body weaken in dazed reaction as her head was forced back by the power of his kiss. Instinctively her hands clutched at him, curling against his bare chest. Response surged through her, as inexorable as the tide, blotting out all thought of struggling free.

It was the sound of a door banging and the thud of footsteps on stairs that tugged them apart. With a muffled curse Armand released her, turning his head as the footsteps came nearer.

Calli stood shaking beside him, not knowing whether to feel relieved or sorry at the interruption.

'Ah, Hamish...it's you.' Armand's voice was perfectly steady, perfectly normal, Calli noted, and it was that, more than anything else, that brought her to her senses. Of course...a little dalliance in the cellar with the young journalist would hardly discompose one so practised in the art of seduction! It would have meant no more to him than that. A moment of dalliance!

'Didn't think you'd still be here.' Hamish looked surprised. 'Or didn't you come straight here after you left me?'

Was he surprised that Armand was still here...or surprised that *she* was with him? Calli wondered.

'We've been sampling,' Armand confessed with a grin that brought a rush of heat to Calli's cheeks. Sampling *what*? Hamish must be wondering. At least Armand hadn't mentioned her naked frolic in the lagoon. She ought to be grateful for that!

With the coolness of one who had only one thing on his mind, Armand reached up to extract a dusty bottle of wine from the rack behind him. 'We'll take a couple of these, I think. And maybe the '76 Hermitage.'

'Leave you to it. I've some work to do,' said Hamish, and vanished round a corner. Calli heard the click of a door being opened and another as it was firmly shut.

'Like to carry these?' Without waiting for her answer, Armand handed her the two bottles. 'I'll carry the others. The Hermitage is along here...' He led the way to another alcove filled with closely stacked bottles. Calli, remembering Stephanie's lost diamond, glanced round while Armand was selecting the bottles he wanted, wondering if it was still down here somewhere. She would need to come down with a torch some time and search around the floor and in the corners...she'd never find it without one.

As she was looking round she noticed a door in a nearby shallow alcove, a shaft of light visible underneath. Obviously the door through which Hamish had vanished a moment ago. She wondered if he worked down here often.

'Coming?' Armand asked with a sharpness that plucked her eyes away from the door. Was he wondering why she was so interested in his cellar?

She walked ahead of him, past the silent rows of bottles and up the narrow cellar steps to a small hinged door at the top, which brought them out into a lobby near the kitchen. Handing Armand the two bottles she had carried for him, she thanked him politely for showing her the cellar, and thankfully made her escape.

At breakfast the next morning Leila greeted her more like a friend than an intrusive journalist, and the smile in Armand's eyes held a sensuous flame that sent a flow of heat through her. She felt a momentary pang of guilt, wondering how Stephanie would feel if she knew she was here—and especially if she knew what a mere look

from Armand, let alone his touch, could do to her, even
mistrusting him the way she did . . . and must always do.
And yet, despite the emotions Armand aroused in her,
and despite the mistrust she still felt for him, and the
guilt and confusion she felt whenever she thought of
Stephanie, she realised that she was happy here at
Château Broch. She had come to genuinely like
Armand's family and the other members of his staff,
and she knew that she would be sorry to leave. For more
reasons than she cared to examine.

'Hey . . . look at this.' Hamish looked up from his
newspaper. 'Roxy Manning and Larry Nicholls have announced their engagement!'

'Really? Well, what do you know!' Leila peered over
his shoulder. 'Not that it should come as a surprise . . . look how chummy they both were when they
were here. They were inseparable. They even shared the
same bedroom. Her bed was never slept in!'

'Leila!' Hamish looked up in mock-reproval. 'You're
not supposed to notice things like that.'

Leila was unrepentant. 'It's all right to say it now that
he's made an honest woman of her. Well, just fancy.
You could say we brought them together.'

While this exchange was going on Calli's eyes were on
Armand's face, looking for the slightest flicker that might
give him away. But all she detected was an amused kind
of acceptance—no embarrassment, no glimmer of guilt,
nothing to suggest he had had a fling with Roxy on the
side, behind her lover's back. She felt puzzled, shaken
by sudden doubts. If Roxy Manning and Larry Nicholls
had been inseparable, how had Armand had the opportunity to take Roxy into his bed? And why would he
have wanted to? Why would Roxy, if she was so crazy
about Larry Nicholls?

Calli bent her head over her breakfast to hide her confusion. Could her sister possibly have been mistaken? Could the girl in Armand's bed have been...some other woman? Not that that would have made it any more bearable for poor Stephanie. Armand had still treated *her* abominably.

She looked up, deciding, in desperation, to take a gamble. 'What a pity you weren't able to bring Stephanie Fox and Armand together as well,' she said teasingly, turning to Leila.

An immediate hush filled the room. Where there had been no tension in the air at the mention of Roxy Manning, now the air was filled with it.

'Yes, well, you can't win 'em all,' Leila said at last, and, with a short laugh, changed the subject.

Calli felt frustrated, but what more could she say without giving herself away? They were determined not to talk about Armand's affair with Stephanie—undoubtedly because they were embarrassed at what Armand had done to her. And she couldn't altogether blame them for being protective. They were Armand's family, and they would hardly want his conduct to be made public.

'I've a couple of overseas phone calls to make,' Armand said, rising from his chair. 'Give me half an hour, Caroline, and then we'll drive down to town to visit Bill in hospital.'

Leila shook her head at him. 'You don't need to, you know. Kurt will visit him.'

Armand shrugged. 'I think we should both pop in whenever we can. Bill's a good man. And it'll give Yvonne a break. They have no other family here, and his workmates will be busy with the vintage. I have to go to town anyway. Davina wants to see me.' He strode out without waiting for comment.

Leila and Hamish wandered off too, and Calli, with half an hour up her sleeve, made a quick decision and went off in search of Agnes. There was one thing she could do for her sister. She could at least try to find her lost diamond!

'Would you have a torch, Agnes?' she asked carelessly, and the woman's brown eyes sharpened.

'A torch? What for?'

'I'd like to pop back down to the cellar for a few moments and look for an earring I must have dropped there last night.'

Agnes seemed to hesitate. 'Does Mr Broch know you're going down there?'

'Mr Broch has given me half an hour while he's busy on the phone.' Calli neatly avoided the question. 'I'll just nip down and see if I can find it. I'd like to wear it tonight when Armand's brother and sister-in-law come for dinner.'

'Well...all right. Over here...' The housekeeper plucked a torch from a shelf in the lobby, and produced a master key from her pocket, unlocking the cellar door and switching on the lights for Calli. As Calli brushed past her she said with a frown, 'You won't be long, will you?'

'I'll be up again the minute I've found it,' Calli assured her, flashing a quick smile. Did the woman think she was planning to steal some of Armand's vintage wines?

She paused on the first narrow stair and pulled the cellar door closed behind her. Even with the lights on, the cellar had a chilling dimness. As she crept down the stairs and passed uneasily between the tall rows of bottles the coldness and the isolation wrapped themselves around her like a physical presence making her flesh crawl. She half expected someone—or *something*—perhaps the ghost of Armand Broch's father or grandfather—to pounce on her in the dimness, and her fingers tightened involuntarily on the torch in her hand, while her other clasped her chest, almost like a shield. But nothing moved, nothing broke the eerie silence. Where to look first? It could be anywhere!

She shone the torch into every corner as she stole along, hoping that the diamond, if it was there, would gleam in the beam of light. After a time, just as she was beginning to despair, she came to the door through which Hamish had vanished last night, and, as she flashed her torch along the grooves at the base, something glistened at her feet. Catching her breath, she bent down to pick it up.

'Bingo!' Hardly believing her luck, she held it up to inspect it. The small familiar stone gleamed in the torch-light. Stephanie would be ecstatic! Calli felt a rush of relief. When her assignment was over and she confessed to Stephanie where she had been this discovery would surely soften the blow of learning that Calli had come here to interview Armand Broch.

Then out of the darkness a deep voice echoed along the corridor of bottles.

'You seem to have a habit of sneaking around the château when you're left alone, Caroline.'

She spun round, aghast. 'Armand! You—you startled me.' As he moved into the pool of light thrown by one of the dangling light-bulbs she took an involuntary step backwards, alarmed at the dangerous fire in his eyes, his granite-hard expression. Shaken, she recalled

Stephanie's pitiful cry, 'I thought he loved me. He's b-broken my heart!'

It gave her the courage to stand up to Armand. Lifting her chin defiantly, she demanded coolly, 'Do you always sneak up on people?'

'Only when I find someone sneaking around,' he returned coldly. 'For all I knew, you could have been an intruder.'

'Didn't Agnes tell you I was down here?' How glad she was that she had had the foresight to let Agnes in on what she was doing!

Armand brushed that aside. 'You're lucky I didn't use this and ask questions afterwards.' He waved a wine bottle at her.

'I'm grateful to you,' she said facetiously. 'You're lucky I didn't hit *you*...with this!' She held up the torch. 'You could have been an intruder yourself. I thought you were busy making phone calls.'

'I was. And as the result of one of them I have invited an extra couple for dinner tonight. An American couple who are in Australia for a visit. I came down to fetch some more wine for dinner.'

Was that the truth, or had Agnes summoned him herself, to let him know that the snoopy journalist was down in his private cellar?

'I came down here to look for an earring I lost last night,' she said, waving her hand at him, with the diamond pressed between her thumb and first finger so that he wouldn't see it too clearly, yet would see that she had indeed found something, hoping he wouldn't remember that she hadn't been wearing earrings the night before—and hoping especially that he wouldn't want to inspect it more closely and see that it wasn't an earring at all, but a diamond from a ring. Stephanie's ring!

She felt her cheeks burning. She was no actress like Stephanie. It was painfully difficult for her to act a part... to lie... to deceive people. And she didn't want to deceive Armand, any more than she was already doing by hiding the fact that she was Stephanie's sister. Despite everything, she wanted him to think well of her—no matter how heartlessly he might have deceived her own sister.

'Armand, I'm sorry if I did the wrong thing by coming down here,' she said contritely.

'Not at all.' His tone was smooth. 'But I would prefer it if in future you came down escorted. You wouldn't want to trip down the stairs or slip in the darkness and have no one down here to come to your aid... would you?'

She looked up at him in bewilderment. That sounded suspiciously like a threat... as if he was saying 'Come down alone again and you'll get hurt!' Now why in the world would he want to resort to threats? Did he honestly believe that she had come down here to steal his precious wine?

'I'm sorry,' she repeated stiffly. 'I'll make sure in future that I don't step out of bounds!'

'Good.' He reached out and checked the door of Hamish's workroom, as if to make sure it was still safely locked. 'Security in a place like this is something one must always be conscious of. I tend to trust my staff— the permanent staff, at any rate. But one can never be too sure about the... casual workers, can one?'

Calli caught her breath. He meant her—he must! The grape-pickers and the other casuals never came down here, as far as she was aware. He was telling her he had his doubts about her... that he couldn't trust her any more!

She felt a wave of despair. And indignation. 'You think I came down here to steal your wine?' she asked huskily, her pale skin stretched tightly across her cheekbones.

He swivelled slowly around to face her, the bare light-bulb above him casting his features into sinister shadow and darkening the deep cleft in his chin. She flinched at the chill light in his eyes—eyes that had turned to green ice, narrowing to slits as they examined her tense face. She shivered, suddenly acutely aware of the cold, un-earthly silence pressing around her, reminding her just how vulnerable she was in this secluded place, alone with Armand Broch—a man whose record showed he had a callous disregard for women!

'Armand, I swear I only came down to find this,' she whispered, waving Stephanie's diamond—not too closely—under his nose. She tossed back her head, adding sarcastically, 'I didn't realise I would be opening Pandora's box by doing that!'

She saw his eyes waver, and, gaining confidence, de-manded recklessly, 'Are you as mistrustful as this with everyone who comes here? How on earth did you manage when you had a whole cast of actors staying here?'

He shot her a quick look, and then gave a sudden bark of laughter, dissolving some of the harsh lines etched in his cheeks. He took her chin in his hand and tilted it upward. 'I don't put you in their category,' he said at length.

She swallowed, an odd pang shooting through her. He had been romantically involved with both of the ac-tresses who had stayed here. Was that what he meant when he said she would never be in their category? As if she didn't know that already!

But that wasn't what all this was about. This was about trust. She raised wide, candid eyes to his. 'I swear I didn't come down here to steal from you, Armand,' she said, a faint tremor in her voice. She couldn't bear it if he thought she had.

His eyes held hers for a long moment, a curious mixture of emotions chasing across his face. 'I wonder if you are as pure and open as you seem?' he said half to himself, his hand sliding down her cheek to encircle her slender neck, his thumb-tip resting lightly on her throat. She felt her own fingers instinctively tighten on the torch in her hand. 'God help you if you're not!'

His face looked grim and dangerous in the shadows, and she trembled at the suppressed passion in his voice. Had he guessed who she was, guessed that she had come here with vengeance in her heart, hoping to expose him for what he had done to her sister? Did she still have vengeance in her heart? Did she still believe he was as cruel, as insensitive as Stephanie had made him out to be? Why wasn't she sure any more? Why did she feel so torn, so confused?

She was conscious of his thumb-tip increasing its pressure on her windpipe. The stark reality of the situation had a strange unreality about it that had a curious effect on her. Suddenly she became deathly calm.

'Armand, would you kindly let go of me?' If her voice sounded slightly unsteady let him put it down to this threatening stance. 'You're behaving very oddly. Would you kindly explain why?' If he suspected who she was let him tell her now, accuse her now!

Abruptly the pressure on her throat eased. His hands dropped to her shoulders and she found she could breathe freely again.

'If you don't know what I'm talking about—and I hope to goodness you don't—then I apologise.'

She swallowed. The hard-edged caution in his voice almost made her burst out with the truth. But the memory of his hands on her throat held her back. How did she know how he might react? In his present mood, if he didn't throttle her on the spot he would almost certainly kick her out. And she couldn't bear the thought of leaving here before she had to. And it wasn't just the thought of her job, or of Stephanie... the truth wasn't as simple as that any more, her reasons too jumbled in her own mind to sort out, especially not right here, right now.

Armand's fingers lingered on her shoulders, while his eyes searched her face, burning with a raw, undefined emotion that sent a tremor through her. 'Heaven knows, I *want* to be able to trust you,' he muttered.

She looked up at him with bruised, vulnerable eyes.

'Oh, Armand... I want you to trust me too!' The words were torn from her. 'And... and I want to trust you!'

At that the expression in his eyes changed, something flaring to life in the green depths. 'Lord, Caroline...' He drove her back against the stone wall, effectively blocking any hope of escape. His eyes were like glowing coals in the dimness. 'If you only knew...' The rest was lost as he buried his lips in the silky mass of her hair. His arms closed around her, crushing her to him, pressing her face into his shirt. Under the smooth cotton she could hear the uneven pounding of his heart and feel the heat of his hard-muscled chest. Response leapt like a flame within her, and any thought of flight melted away.

He breathed into her ear, 'Caroline, I'm sorry... I do trust you... forgive me!'

She felt his hand come up under her chin, his touch like the sizzle of an electric charge on her fiery skin. He lifted his head for a brief moment and brought it down again, running a line of tiny kisses along her hairline, then dragged his lips in one sensuous motion along her temple, down the curve of her cheek to her lips.

She whimpered softly as she felt the warm compelling movement of his mouth on hers. Feeling her response, he deepened his kiss, his mouth opening over hers, his tongue moistening her soft lips, prising them apart, probing, circling, thrusting deep inside.

Her body arched instinctively, her breasts swelling and throbbing, his closeness bringing an immediate response from every nerve-cell in her body. As she ran her arms up his back the torch in her hand slipped from her nerveless fingers.

The sound of metal striking stone was like an explosion in the silence, shocking her back to sanity. She tore her mouth from his, seeing a vision of Stephanie's agonised face, her lovely dark eyes wounded—and puzzled. 'I've lost everything now...everything I ever wanted!' her sister had wailed. What was she thinking of—Stephanie's own sister—inviting Armand's kisses?

'The torch!' she gasped, twisting away from him as mortification flooded through her. Why, oh, why had she numbly responded to him? Why hadn't she resisted?

'Forget the torch!' Armand's hands swung her back to face him. 'Don't turn away from me, Caroline. Haven't I just proved to you that I trust you, believe you?' He shook her gently. 'Why do you have this effect on me, you wide-eyed little temptress? You only have to look at me...' She heard the thickness in his voice and saw in the pearly dimness the burning desire in his eyes as he tried to recapture her lips. 'You want this as much as I do...swear to me that you don't!'

'Want *what*?' she flung back at him, seizing on anger to hide her pain. His assurance, his arrogance, his assumption that she wanted him as much as he wanted her had touched her on the raw. 'An affair? Is that what you mean? Or just a harmless dalliance with the gullible young journalist... with her willing participation, of course?'

A spasm crossed his face. Was it guilt? Anger? Pain? 'You still don't trust me, do you, Caroline? *Can't* you trust me?' he pleaded, his hands tightening on her arms. 'Haven't I just shown that I trust *you*?'

She mustn't listen! 'Oh, don't patronise me!' she flared, struggling away from him and pointedly running her hand across her lips. Armand Broch gave his kisses so freely—so unthinkingly! They meant nothing to him. When one woman's kisses palled he merely looked for another's!

'You think that's what I was doing when I kissed you? Patronising you?' There was a rough edge now to his voice. 'You enjoyed it as much as I did!'

Colour flooded her cheeks. 'Well, I——' she bit her lip '—I'd rather you didn't...do it again, Armand. I don't believe in—in meaningless gestures of that sort.'

'Neither do I.'

She eyed him with scorn. 'You have a reputation,' she reminded him boldly, 'for changing your women as often as your shirts. That sounds pretty meaningless to me. You admitted yourself that you have shared your bed on numerous occasions.'

He gave a sudden bark of laughter. 'There's no comparison! You, my sweet Caroline, are as far removed from those women as Venus is from Earth.'

Was that intended as an insult or a compliment? Calli eyed him uncertainly. 'Aren't you forgetting Davina?' she rallied.

'No.' His tone was bantering now. 'I'm not forgetting Davina.'

'*Ooh!*' she growled, glaring up at him. He was still standing far too close. 'Aren't we supposed to be going into town?' she reminded him tremulously, reaching up to smooth her hair.

'We are.' Was that a faint sigh? 'You have a strange effect on me, Caroline. I don't know what it is about you.'

'I'm a woman—that's all it is,' she flung back tartly—if a trifle breathlessly. 'I'll just run up to my room and grab my camera.'

'Don't you want the torch?' He swooped down to pick it up. 'It's still working. Here...take it.'

'Thank you,' she gasped, snatching it and stumbling away from him.

His voice drifted after her, tinged with amusement. 'I'll meet you at the car.'

This has just been a game to him, she decided, her fingers clenching round the metal torch—seizing on anger to stifle other emotions that were threatening to swamp her. He's a past master at games, at fooling women. When will you ever learn?

Bill Dysan had been moved from Intensive Care into one of the general wards. Armand sent Yvonne away to have a break while he sat and chatted with Bill. Finding Bill in good spirits, he beckoned Calli in to join them.

'No need to take a photograph,' Armand muttered, but Bill had other ideas.

'You take one, Caroline. No one knows what Armand does for his staff, because he never advertises it.'

'The public doesn't need to know,' Armand growled. 'I'm prepared to publicise my business dealings, but my private life is just that—private.' Was it just accidental that he was avoiding her eye? Calli pondered, her eyes narrowing. He would hardly want her to advertise what had happened down in his private cellar!

'That's why there is so much false speculation about you,' Bill teased, emboldened perhaps by the fact that he was encased in bandages and plaster. 'If people don't know the truth there's always someone who will make it up. And not always in your favour.'

Calli spoke up then, jutting out her chin. 'I've tried to tell Armand that myself. People love to read about . . . what makes a man tick, how he thinks, how he sees the women in his life . . .'

'I'm not going to apologise for not being the kiss-and-tell type.' Armand's lip lifted wryly. 'A gentleman doesn't talk about his *affaires d'amour*. However, should my personal situation ever change and . . . stabilise—shall we say?—then that might be a different story.'

Calli swallowed. Was he referring to Davina? He must be! Davina had asked to see him this morning. To finally give him her answer? Had Armand at last decided to settle down? Had this morning been simply a last fling?

Why did her spirits dip at the prospect of Armand finally deciding to settle down . . . with Davina? Was she thinking of Stephanie, who had loved Armand to distraction—who might love him still and be hoping to win him back, for all she knew? Or was she thinking of . . . ? No, she was *not*! That hadn't meant a thing. Not to him . . . and not to her! And she'd be crazy to think any different!

They had barely walked in the door of Armand's riverside restaurant when a breathlessly excited Davina hurled herself into Armand's arms. Calli would have been blind not to notice the gleaming sapphire and diamond ring on her third finger. She felt as if a knife were twisting inside her. Damn it, Calli, you were expecting this—get a grip on yourself!

Dazed as she was, she managed to raise her camera and catch the happy moment.

'Oh, Armand, it *worked*,' Davina squealed as she extricated herself from Armand's embrace. 'He's agreed! And look...' she thrust her ring under his nose '...it's official! We're getting married in a month.'

Calli felt the room tilt under her feet. *What* had worked? Who was *he*? What did she mean, '*We're* getting married in a month'?

'Well done! This deserves a toast!' Armand was beaming, looking as happy as Davina. But how...why...?

'There's just time to share a glass with you before the lunch crowd arrives.' Davina clicked her fingers and a figure hovering behind snapped into action. 'I see you still have your young shadow, Armand...' Davina threw Calli a glance as they moved to one of the tables, and in the second that their eyes met Calli had the feeling Davina was seeing more than she ought to see. She managed to pull herself together and force a smile as she offered her congratulations.

'Armand, I hope you are taking good care of this girl,' Davina scolded gently. 'You just have to look at her to see that she's not your usual cynical, hardened journalist—the type who puts her story before everything else. Come to that, she's nothing like the women you normally have around you. I saw that the first time I met her. I just hope *you're* aware of it, darling.'

Calli sucked in a quivering breath. Davina seemed to be warning Armand to keep his hands off her, warning him not to take advantage of her. She recalled the previous warning Davina had made the first time they had met. She had thought then that Davina was warning her off because she had wanted Armand for herself. But now it seemed that she had been warning her to beware of Armand because of his reputation with women! Davina was afraid she might end up getting hurt.

It's all right, Davina, I had my sister to warn me, Calli reflected ruefully. And poor fool me, I haven't heeded either of your warnings, because I do feel something for Armand, and I don't seem to be able to repress it. And if I end up getting hurt it's my own fault! And I will, because there's no future in it, I *know* that!

'You have no need to worry, Davina, my pet,' Armand said, and to Calli's embarrassment he was now looking at *her*, not at Davina, and the *way* he was looking at her made her legs feel quite weak. 'I intend to take good care of her. I'm not the ogre you seem to think me.'

'Of course you're not.' Davina flashed him a smile. 'Though David thinks you are, the way you forced me to hold out until we had resolved where we were going to live!'

Armand looked anything but repentant as he said with a grin, 'So he's agreed to settle here in Adelaide?'

'He has. And he'll commute to Sydney when he needs to. It means I can go on running the restaurant. I'm so pleased about that!'

'I know that's what you wanted,' Armand said calmly. He turned back to Calli, explaining, 'Davina's fiancé is a Sydney businessman. But most of his business is here in Adelaide—he's always flying down here, and not just to see Davina. I persuaded Davina to persuade *him* to come and settle here in Adelaide, and commute to Sydney when necessary. Why should the woman always be the one to follow the man?'

As the three of them raised their glasses Calli shook her head in self-reproach. It all made sense now. Why Armand had said he *needed* Davina . . . why he had said he intended to be very *persuasive*. She had got it all wrong!

What else might she have got wrong about him? she wondered now. Was it conceivable that Stephanie too might have interpreted things wrongly? Armand's proposal of marriage . . . her sister's conviction that he loved her . . . Could Stephanie possibly have jumped to conclusions, read more into their affair than Armand had intended?

She had to find out! *Facts*, Calli. They have to be dead accurate, remember?

'Before we go to the airport to pick up our American friends I want to pop into the branch office for half an hour or so,' Armand said as they drove away from the restaurant after a pleasant lunch together. It gave Calli the opportunity she had been waiting for.

'While you're there would you mind if I nipped out and did a couple of things in town? I'd only need half an hour.'

'Sure, why not? The office is just around the corner from Rundle Street Mall . . . handy for any of the department stores. Just come back to the office when you're ready—I'll wait for you.'

She didn't tell him it wasn't shopping that she had in mind, but making a couple of interstate phone calls. She hadn't wanted to make them from the château in case her calls were overheard.

She had no trouble finding a secluded phone box. She dialled Stephanie's number, and when there was no answer she rang her sister's agent to see if Stephanie was

still filming, though she should have finished by now
and be taking a well-earned break. Calli hadn't told
Stephanie where she would be this week, of course—she
had simply said that she would be away for a few days
on an assignment, and would be in touch when she got
back.

'She's gone away,' Stephanie's agent told her. 'She
wanted a few days' rest in the sun before taking on anything else. She went up to the Gold Coast, I think.'

'You *think*? You mean she didn't leave you a number?'
That didn't sound like Stephanie. Calli felt a flutter of
alarm. Had her sister gone into seclusion again? Did that
mean she still wasn't over Armand?

'She did, but apparently she's moved out again. Maybe
she's on her way back home already. Want me to get her
to ring you when I catch up with her?'

'No, don't bother—I'll be moving around... I'll try
again later. Thanks, Joe.'

She hung up, feeling none the wiser about Stephanie's
frame of mind—or about anything else she had wanted
to find out. The questions she had wanted to ask about
Roxy Manning, and about Armand, would just have to
wait.

She took the opportunity to say hello to her parents
and also to ring Howie at the office, just to report in.
Then she rang Julie, the young mother who lived in the
flat next door, who was collecting her mail, and quickly
ascertained that nothing had come from Stephanie, and
no other urgent mail was waiting for her.

When she met up again with Armand he looked
surprised.

'What, no parcels? I thought you were going
shopping.'

'I... couldn't find what I wanted. So I made a few phone calls instead.'

'You can always ring from the château, you know. Any time.'

'That's kind of you, Armand. But these were personal calls... interstate. I'm sure you wouldn't want me tying up your phone on long-distance calls to all and sundry.'

'Don't be ridiculous, Caroline. You can ring your family whenever you want to. You can ring...anywhere.' She noted the way he paused before that thoughtful 'anywhere'; heard at the same time a new note creep into his voice. And something about the way he was looking at her now sent a coil of unease through her.

Had he guessed she had been making calls she didn't want him to overhear? Was he wondering *why* she was being so secretive?

She felt like kicking herself. Why had she mentioned the phone calls in the first place? Why couldn't she be cleverer at pretending, making up stories? She sighed, knowing perfectly well why: it just wasn't *her*. How she wished all this secrecy and subterfuge were over! How she wished she had never started it! What she wouldn't give to be plain old Calli Smith again, with no secrets, no need to watch her every word, no niggling worries about her sister! At the same time, contrarily, she was beginning to quite like being called Caroline. The way Armand said it at times made it sound almost like a... caress.

But the way he was looking at her now made her heart sink. Would she ever hear that soft, caressing note in his voice again?

There was no time to brood, because within minutes they were at the airport, and once they had their overseas visitors in the car—a jovial middle-aged couple from the

Napa Valley in California, Mickey and Dale O'Rourke—
the drive back to the Barossa Valley passed in a whirl
of chatter, laughter and a lively exchange of ideas about
wine production, with Armand pointing out scenic points
of interest along the way. He slowed the car when they
reached the Barossa wine district, meandering past a
number of wineries, giving a brief run-down on each
one until finally they swept through the gates of Château
Broch.

Calli sat forward in her seat. And, for the first time
since they had left town, Armand let his gaze collide
briefly with hers... and in that fleeting collision she
glimpsed a spark of the softness she had seen there
before. But as his eyes veered away she was left with the
flickering impression of something else. Was there the
faintest query there as well?

CHAPTER NINE

As THEY stepped from the car two small girls in blue jeans and T-shirts burst from the shade of the poplars and hurled themselves at Armand, squealing, 'Uncle Armand, Uncle Armand!'

Calli, snatching up her camera, caught Armand just as he was swinging the smaller of the two girls high into the air, while the other clung to his leg, shrieking, 'I want to fly too, I want to fly too!'

Armand's face had come alive, Calli noted, giving her a glimpse of yet another side of him. It was plain the two little girls adored him, equally plain that he felt the same about them. So, she mused dazedly...he even loves children. So many things about Armand are so *good*, and yet... She sighed. The spectre of Stephanie and what Armand had done to her was always there, nagging away at her, showing her a darker side that he and his family were being careful to keep hidden from her.

A young woman emerged from the shadows, an older version of the two girls, with the same tumbling curls, the same dancing blue eyes. Armand, with a child now balanced on each arm, introduced her as Amy, wife of his brother Kurt, whom they were to meet shortly afterwards. Kurt, considerably slighter than his strapping brother, had his twin sister Leila's lean face and dark eyes—the same dark eyes Calli had seen in their father in the portrait gallery upstairs. Armand's unusual green eyes must have come from their mother. The mother that he had never mentioned, other than a curtly dismissive, 'She's dead.'

Calli, even with her camera at hand, was made to feel like one of the family at dinner that evening, a fun get-together with Château Broch wines flowing freely. The two little girls, bathed and fed and already in their pyjamas, were allowed to join them briefly before dinner, and it was Armand, Calli noticed, who took them up to bed. Both girls squealingly demanded it, and Armand obliged without turning a hair. When he came down again Leila had already seated everyone at the table.

Calli found herself placed between Armand, at the head of the table, and their American visitor, Mickey O'Rourke. Armand, now that he was no longer besieged by his young nieces, seemed to notice Calli for the first time. She felt his gaze dwell for a moment on her face, and then flicker downward, making the fine hairs on her arms prickle in response.

'You're looking particularly lovely tonight, Caroline.'

She tried not to over-react to the compliment. He was seeing her dressed up for the first time, that was all. She had taken extra pains tonight because it was a special dinner, washing her hair and brushing it until it shone, leaving it flowing loose, framing her delicate oval face like a silky cloud. And she was wearing one of her favourites, a deceptively simple cream dress, nipped in at the waist and flaring to her knees, a dress that she knew flattered her fair complexion and showed off her long slender legs. Mindful of what she had told Agnes earlier in the day, she had remembered to wear earrings, choosing the small diamond and pearl ones her parents had given her for her twenty-first.

'Thank you,' she said as calmly as she could. 'You look pretty good yourself.' An understatement! Armand, his wide shoulders and slim hips accentuated by his well-cut navy sports jacket, his green eyes compelling under a lock of wavy dark hair, looked magnificent. When he had walked in she had felt her throat constrict, his easy grace, his powerful physique, his almost saturnine attractiveness leaving her faintly breathless.

'Yes, Caroline does look lovely this evening,' put in Leila, overhearing her brother's remark. 'You'd never think she has been on the go all day. At least I've had a rest—Hamish insisted on it. I've been luxuriating in a hot bath for the past two hours!'

'Well, it's done you good—you look wonderful too, Leila.' Armand ran approving eyes over his sister, elegant in draped red jersey, the rich shade a dramatic foil for her dark colouring. 'In fact, you look radiant. I do believe you've put a bit of flesh on those far too slender bones of yours. And you look better for it.'

Leila and Hamish exchanged glances.

'Shall we tell them?' Leila's dark eyes were sparkling in a way Calli had never seen before. She looked as though she would burst if she didn't speak out.

'It was you who wanted to keep it a secret,' Hamish reminded her, his own pale eyes filled with an emotion as powerful as Leila's. 'After the vintage, you said...when things quieten down a bit and we're quite *sure*...that would be soon enough to tell everyone.'

'We *are* quite sure,' said Leila, bubbling over. 'And I can't keep it to myself any longer!'

'You mean——?' Armand's mouth had dropped open in a flash of comprehension, and when Leila and Hamish nodded the whole table erupted in delight.

'How wonderful! Congratulations! *When*, Leila?'

'Around Christmas,' Leila confessed, her eyes shining. 'We're both so thrilled and excited. Having a baby at

last! Armand, we're going to buy a house. We know the
one we want already—the Grants' old place. It's coming
up for auction in about three weeks and we're going to
make an offer beforehand to make sure we get it. It's
close enough to Château Broch for Hamish to come and
go each day, and I'll go on working too for as long as
I can.'

'You don't have to go rushing out to buy another
house,' Armand said with a faint frown. 'There's plenty
of room here... surely? We're not exactly falling over
one another.'

'You know we always said we'd find a place of our
own when we started a family,' Hamish put in. 'Old
Grant's place has come on the market at just the right
time, God rest his crusty old soul. It's an ideal family
home—it'll suit us just fine.'

'Just as Château Broch will be perfect for you and
your own family, Armand, one day,' Leila put in softly.
'One day soon, perhaps? I have high hopes for you, big
brother,' she added, laughing across the table at him.
Calli glanced at Armand. If Davina was now out of the
picture then... who could Leila mean? Armand was
giving nothing away, an enigmatic smile on his lips, but,
when she glanced back at Leila, Leila was looking at
her, her dark eyes dancing in a way that left no doubt
where her hopes lay!

Calli sucked in an astonished breath, a flush staining
her cheeks, and for one crazy, irrational second she felt
a quiver of some deeply buried, barely formed hope of
her own—until she came back to reality and quickly
buried it back where it belonged. Even if Armand was
not the monster Stephanie had made him out to be, even
if he believed in marriage and commitment, even if he
came truly to care for her, what good were hopes? Just

frothy dreams, fairy-tales! And fairy-tales didn't come true for wicked deceivers... let alone for obscure little journalists, just passing through.

The evening was such a lively affair from that moment on that Calli was soon sailing along with them, and joining in the fun. When they moved into the lounge for coffee Amy seized her chance to slip out and check on the girls. Calli hesitated, debating whether she ought to excuse herself too and leave the family and their American guests to themselves. Just as she had decided to take her leave she saw Armand stiffen and turn towards the window.

'What are those dogs barking at?'

'Possums, most likely,' Hamish said unworriedly, flopping into an armchair, a glass of port in his hand.

'No... it's more than that. They're going mad about something.' Armand moved towards the door. 'I'm going out to check.'

'I'll come with you,' said Kurt, and Calli snatched up her camera and followed them out, dimly aware that Hamish was hauling himself out of his deep armchair.

The cool air hit them as they raced outside. There was no moon tonight—thin wisps of cloud had been floating in all day, thickening into a smooth grey blanket overhead. A sharp wind had sprung up, and the temperature had dropped dramatically.

'I smell smoke,' Kurt said, and Armand shouted,

'Look over there!' A faint red glow showed through the trees. 'Hell! It's the storage shed—it's chock-full of new cartons and labels and heaven knows what else! Worse, all our archives are in there! We can't lose those.' He snapped over his shoulder, 'Caroline, get Leila to call the fire brigade! Kurt, you get the fire hose. I'll go and take a look!'

'Be careful!' Calli begged. She stumbled back inside, gasped out what had happened, and as Leila flew to the phone she tore outside again, gripping her camera as she pounded across the darkened yard.

She could hear an ominous crackling and roaring, and when she reached the storage shed she saw that one end of the long wooden building was already well alight. She heard the sound of breaking glass and saw yellow flames licking through the open window. Running around to the doorway, she was just in time to see Kurt dragging in a huge hose, bellowing at Hamish to turn on the water. As it came spurting out he vanished inside.

'Where's Armand?' Calli shrieked, running through the open doorway, almost colliding with Armand as he came tottering out with an armload of boxes.

'Caroline, get back—the whole place could go up any minute! Get your damned photographs from a safe distance!' He threw the boxes outside, some bursting on impact, spewing papers, as he swung on his heel and plunged back into the burning shed.

Hamish appeared behind her, and pushed past her, diving towards the rear of the shed. 'Our whole history is in those archives! We've got to save them!'

'My God!' The cry came from Mickey O'Rourke, who had burst out of the darkness. 'What are they doing in there? They'll kill themselves! Caroline, what do you think you're doing?'

Calli, throwing down her camera, shrieked over her shoulder, 'Armand needs all the help he can get!' and, with her hand shielding her face from the heat, she streaked through the doorway, leaping over the hose and dodging piles of boxes as she ran. She gave a cry when she saw Armand, half hidden by smoke, plunging towards the flames, grabbing the hose from Kurt, who staggered back, as if overcome by the heat or the fumes. She had a vivid image of Armand's tall figure silhouetted against the flames, with burning timber supports all around him as he stood his ground, pointing a gushing stream of water at the licking flames.

She screamed as one of the timber supports gave way, almost crashing on top of him. She gabbled a silent prayer while she darted forward and caught Kurt's arm as he reeled towards her.

'You've got to get some air, Kurt!' She dragged him to the doorway and pushed him into Mickey's waiting arms. Then she turned back, rushing to the small room at the rear of the shed, where she almost collided with Hamish as he staggered out with a load of boxes.

'Caroline, what the hell do you think you're doing in here?'

'Give me those boxes—you go and get some more!' She almost dragged them from his arms, stumbled under their weight as she turned and staggered back to the door, where Mickey was ready to take them from her. They now had a chain, an assembly line of sorts, and within minutes, though it felt more like hours, all the vital papers had been retrieved.

They heard a crash as another support caved in.

'Armand, get out—*quick*!' Hamish bellowed. 'The roof's going!' At the same time the roar of a siren announced the arrival of the fire brigade—two fire trucks, in fact, with hoses quickly in action. Armand just escaped from the burning building as the roof fell in. His face was blackened, his shirt torn, his hair slightly tinged. But he was safe!

'We got out all we needed to, Armand!' Hamish flung his arm round his brother-in-law's shoulders. 'The store's gone, but it doesn't matter now.' Their biggest fear was that the fire would spread to the adjoining building, where hundreds of bottles, already labelled and ready for distribution, were stored. But within minutes they knew it was safe. The fire trucks had the fire under control.

There was a lot of talking, all at once. Leila, Amy and Dale O'Rourke were there too, their faces showing their relief as they crowded around their menfolk.

Armand's head jerked round. 'Where's Caroline?'

Caroline swallowed. 'Here I am, Armand.' She knew she must look a real fright if her face was as blackened as his. She reached up, knowing her hair must be a mess, and her cream dress, she realised now as she ran her gaze over it for the first time, was ruined!

Armand was frowning at her. 'I thought I told you to keep away. You got some good shots?'

She bit her lip, quick colour heating her cheeks. The best shots all week, and she'd missed them! She could have shown Armand in action, as the hero he was. Now all she could do was describe the scene. Not quite the same as graphic pictures! 'Oh, Armand, I'm sorry! I— I didn't think...'

'Caroline is a real heroine,' Kurt put in, catching her arm and dragging her forward. 'She rescued me, and then she organised a chain to get all the stuff out. She wasn't in there taking photographs!'

Armand's gaze veered round to rest on her face, his eyes glimmering in the darkness with an expression she couldn't read. Was he going to be angry that she had ignored his order to stay away?

'You mean...you forgot about your assignment and rushed in there, just to help us?' His tone was bemused, and a trifle husky. 'Where *is* your camera?' he asked after a pause.

'Here's her camera,' Mickey said from behind. 'I picked it up from where she dropped it.' He grinned. 'I think it's still in one piece, though.'

'Some journalist,' Hamish muttered teasingly. 'Tossing away your camera at the vital moment.'

None of them *sounded* cross. But they must be disappointed. She had fallen down on her job.

'Let me take a photograph now,' she begged, reaching for her camera. Armand's hand closed on her arm.

'Forget the damned camera,' he said, just as Mickey piped up in his Californian drawl,

'I have a confession to make. I'm a camera buff myself, and *I* took a few shots for Caroline. You wouldn't have noticed the flash, what with the fire 'n all.'

'Well, well...there you are, Caroline, you haven't missed out on anything, after all.' Armand's hand was on her shoulder now, his fingers gently stroking her nape, sending a shivery sensation down her spine, a quite delicious feeling. 'Leila, take Caroline back to the house, will you? Get Agnes to make her some tea or something. And then you'd better clean yourself up, Caroline, and go to bed. We'll mop up here. I want to find out how the fire started in the first place.' For a second his fingers wound themselves in her hair, drawing her fractionally closer. 'Thank you, Caroline. Don't think we don't appreciate what you did. Go on, now. And have a good night's sleep.'

'You too, Armand. Goodnight, everyone!'

*   *   *

The next day passed in a flurry of activity. Insurance assessors arrived, and the police, and reporters, and after sifting through the burnt-out remains of the storage shed, with nothing suspicious being found, and no electrical fault coming to light, the cause of the fire was put down to a slowly smouldering cigarette butt, most likely dropped there earlier in the day by one of the truck-drivers who had delivered material for storage there.

Armand's secretary Lauren joined Calli at one point during the morning, when she came out to look over the damage.

'Believe you're the heroine of the piece,' the tall redhead remarked with a friendly smile. 'You're making quite an impression here, Caroline, one way and another.'

There was something in her tone that made Calli look at her quickly. 'Meaning?'

'Meaning I've heard nothing but praise all week—from Leila, from Hamish, from Armand.'

'From Armand?'

'Sure. But it's not what he's said so much—it's his tone of voice whenever he's mentioned you, the look in his eye. He's normally pretty blasé where women are concerned. But with you, Caroline, he's different. I can see the change in him. *Hear* it.'

'You know him that well?' Just how close had they been in the past? And why should it matter to her?

'Yes, I know him pretty well. But not the way you're thinking—I have a long-time boyfriend of my own.' The girl's eyes twinkled. 'You have very expressive eyes, Caroline. You're stuck on him, aren't you?'

Calli's heart jumped. 'Is it that obvious?' Dear lord, why had she said that? Why hadn't she denied it? She tried to laugh it off. 'Senseless, isn't it? I've known him a few days . . . and I never intended——' She broke off, waving her hands. What was it about this girl that was making her say things she had tried not to admit even to herself? 'Anyway, I'll be gone in a couple of days. Don't say anything, Lauren—please! It can't come to anything...' And that wasn't what she had meant to say either! 'I'll get over it,' she muttered. But *would* she?

Lauren squeezed her arm. 'Don't worry—your secret is safe with me. But what makes you think it won't come to anything? He likes you too, I know he does. I wouldn't be at all surprised if he wants to go on seeing you... I mean, after you've finished your job here.'

Calli looked away. 'No... it's impossible.'

'*Why* is it? You're a lovely girl, Caroline. You're so warm and natural—beautiful, too. And bright. I've read your stuff—you're good... yet you don't push yourself forward. You're compassionate, you think of other people... and you don't put your job before everything else—I heard what you did last night. You're a really nice girl, Caroline.'

A girl who's been deceiving your boss all the week... a girl whose own sister suffered at your boss's hands. Aloud Calli said pensively, 'Armand's not going to get himself tied up with me. I'm an old-fashioned girl—I believe in love and marriage. Commitment.'

'Give the guy a chance. I'm sure he believes in those things too... with the right girl.'

Calli drew in a ragged breath. 'I heard he was tied up with Stephanie Fox while she was here... that he'd asked *her* to marry him—not long before they broke up.'

'Never!' Lauren sounded quite adamant. 'They had a bit of a fling, that was all—*she* chased after Armand. I saw her in action with my own eyes. He didn't want to have a bar of her at first—he has this thing about actresses... he loathes them. But she wore him down in the end. I guess he thought—what the heck? It's only a bit of fun. And she *was* a real dish—what man could resist her?'

Calli swallowed. 'But I heard she was crazy about him. She wanted to *marry* him. She was devastated when it broke up.'

'You mean she's been talking about it?' Lauren looked surprised. 'I thought they'd made an agreement not to. Look, there was never any question of marriage, or anything serious. Armand would never get stuck on an actress. He'd certainly never marry one. I told you, he doesn't trust them an inch.'

'Why doesn't he?'

'Because his own mother was an actress. She ran out on Armand's father when Armand and Leila and Kurt were only kids. She'd had an offer to go to Hollywood, and couldn't resist it. The offers came to nothing, apparently, and she went into a quick slide downhill. But she wouldn't come home. She ended up dying of an overdose. No one ever knew if it was accidental or deliberate. Armand's father never remarried...he was a broken, bitter man to the day he died. Armand's never forgiven his mother for the way she ran out on them...for the way she destroyed his father.'

'And he's never trusted a woman since?' Calli asked softly. 'Is that why he's never stuck for long with any one woman?'

'Maybe. But I think he trusts *you*, Caroline. Maybe the right woman's just never come along...until now.'

'I told you...it won't happen. Not Armand and me.' Calli felt a lump rising in her throat. How long would his trust last when he found out that she had been deceiving him about who she was? And how could she ever trust *him*, after the way he had hurt her sister? 'Lauren, you won't——'

She didn't need to finish. 'I won't say anything, I promise. I'm a confidential secretary, remember? I'm used to keeping confidences.'

'Thank you.' Calli touched her arm gratefully. 'I really appreciate it.'

Lauren had the last word. 'Good luck,' she said, and the twinkle was back in her eye. Calli merely shook her head.

After lunch Kurt drove off with his family, taking the O'Rourkes with them to look over his McLaren Vale vineyard. As the others waved them off Armand frowned up at the sky. The clouds were thickening and growing darker, and the temperature had dropped even further, bringing with it an icy cold wind. For the first time all week they were wearing sweaters.

'Storm clouds,' Armand muttered. 'Anyone hear a forecast?'

'Yes, there's a storm coming all right—in fact, they're forecasting hailstorms this evening,' Hamish said with a grimace. 'I just heard on the radio.'

'*Hail!* Damn! One more day and we would have picked all the grapes. There are only the palaminos left to bring in.' The palamino grapes, Calli had learned over lunch, were the large dark green vigorous-growing grapes used in the production of high-quality dry sherry.

Armand made a snap decision. 'We're all going to have to jump to it and strip those palamino grapes off the vines—in a hurry. I don't want to risk having them damaged now. Spread the word around—I want every pair of hands we can get! All pickers who'll stay on after their normal finishing time today will be paid double.

And anyone from the winery who'll lend a hand will be paid a bonus too.'

'I'd like to help too,' Calli offered at once.

Armand grabbed her hands. 'With these?' He stroked her soft palms for a second with the tips of his fingers, then let them go, shaking his head. 'Look, if you want to help you can keep the pickers supplied with empty containers.'

Calli stood her ground. 'You have young kids to do that.' She had seen the pickers' children hauling the containers around. 'I thought you needed all the hands you could get? I have perfectly useful hands, Armand.'

'Well . . . OK.' He touched her briefly on the arm. 'I haven't time to argue—let's get moving! Stay close to me!'

They all leapt into action—Armand, Hamish, Lauren and one or two others from the office, even Leila and a couple of her helpers from the tasting-room, leaving a skeleton staff behind to keep the place going until closing time.

Armand rapped instructions at Calli and the others who were new to the task. 'Only do the grapes on your side of the wire. Don't go wrecking your hands by pulling and tugging. Pull the branches back—like this. And snip here—like this. And before you move on make sure you haven't left any good fruit on the vines.'

They set to work, feverishly snipping off the ripe grapes in bunches, as Armand had shown them, and dropping them into containers, which when full were gathered up by the big trailers.

'Take care,' Armand muttered anxiously as he watched Calli take a thick bunch of grapes into her hand, the grapes firm and ripe, ready to burst with their load of sweet juices. 'Don't chop your fingers off with those cutters.'

'I won't.' Calli clicked her razor-sharp secateurs, and grinned at him. She had taken one quick photograph of Armand before dumping her camera under the vines to retrieve later.

It was hard work—hard on the arms, shoulders and back, and harder still on the hands. Calli had never worked so hard or so fast in her life. And yet she found herself enjoying it. Each time she filled a container she felt an enormous sense of satisfaction and achievement. When, she wondered idly, had she ever felt so good, so alive, so *needed*, back at the newspaper office? The noisy, cluttered office seemed so shadowy and remote, so *humdrum* from this distance. This is where I want to be, she realised with a jolt. This is where I feel happiest.

Was it because Armand was there, working closely, industriously beside her, warming her with words and smiles of encouragement?

'You may taste the merchandise, you know,' he said at one point. 'It'll help if you're feeling thirsty.'

Gratefully she crammed a mouthful of grapes into her mouth, and felt them burst against her palate and the juice run down her throat. They were deliciously sweet, with faint overtones of sourness in the skins.

As the sky grew ominously darker the wind picked up, rustling the vines and causing the leaves to slap her in the face and the long canes to tangle in her hair. Rather than slowing down, she stepped up her pace, aware that time must be running out. Her forefingers were getting sore, and there was a crick in her back, but she closed her mind to the pain. It would pass. It was just that she wasn't used to it.

Armand's voice came from close by. 'Try kneeling down to pick the lower ones—it's easier on the back.'

She knelt gratefully in the reddish-brown earth, dragging the container she was filling along with her as she moved. She was kneeling in crushed grapes, and she was thirsty again, but she had a smile on her lips. She had settled into the rhythm of the picking, and was finding satisfaction in the clean snip-snap of the stems as they were cut, the comfortable thud of the bunches into the bin at her side. She hardly noticed Hamish approaching until he spoke.

'Armand, I wonder if you would come and speak to Leila. She's looking done in but she refuses to stop. I'm afraid she'll keel over any minute.'

'I'll come and talk to her.' Armand straightened. 'I'll tell her that if she keels over two others at least will have to stop work to look after her. That should get through to her. I'll ask her to organise some drinks—that way she can still help out.'

'Thanks, old man. And Lauren has to leave too in a few minutes. She has a sporting commitment in Nuriootpa this evening that she can't get out of.'

'I'll see her and thank her before she goes.'

Before he left he came and rested a hand lightly on Calli's shoulder. 'You take care while I'm gone. I don't want anything happening to those precious fingers of yours.'

She stared after him, an image of his warm smile and the tenderness in his eyes lingering in her mind as he swung away. 'Precious', he'd said.

How would she ever be able to bear leaving here? Leaving *him*? It was no use pretending any longer. She *loved* Armand. Despite everything, despite Stephanie, despite knowing it was futile, and that such a thing couldn't have happened so quickly...she knew it was true. She loved him! She fumbled with the bunch of grapes in her hand, her mind drifting for a mad moment into the area of dreams.

Careful, Calli, you fool...do you want to cut off your fingers? Your *precious* fingers? He only called them precious because he knows you need them to write with, to take photographs with...not because they are precious to *him*. Concentrate on what you are doing, or you'll be the next casualty.

Her face was so intent when Armand came back that she didn't notice him straight away. Not until his hand gently closed over the secateurs in her hand, making sure they were out of harm's way before he spoke.

'I'm back,' he said, his rich voice rolling through her. 'You looked so engrossed that I was afraid you'd jump and cut yourself if I spoke or started snipping beside you.'

She looked up at him, and saw a look in his eyes that made her own veer away in panic, her gaze fastening on the smooth lock of dark hair tumbling across his brow, studying it as if it were the most intriguing thing about him. In truth, her fingers itched to slide through its silky softness, to take his face in her hands and bring those sensuous lips down on her own so that she could taste them and... Calli Smith, what are you thinking of?

She dropped her gaze, wondering ruefully how she must look to him, her hair a mess, her lipstick worn off, her face shiny and sweat-streaked, her legs and arms scratched.

His fingers trailed up her arm and he rubbed his thumb in circles on the ball of her shoulder. 'Are you OK?'

'I'm fine.' The tenderness in his voice was almost her undoing. How could she ever bear to leave this place, to leave *him*? The very thought caused a sick, sinking feeling inside her. She simply couldn't believe any longer that Armand was the heartless monster that Stephanie had made him out to be. The man she had come to know was no monster. He was caring, trustworthy, high-principled and honest. A *good* man. Stephanie must have been over-reacting, she decided. Being theatrical. It wouldn't be the first time.

'We're on the last leg,' Armand said encouragingly. 'With luck, we'll have the vines stripped completely before that hailstorm hits. You're doing a great job, Caroline. But you're to stop if you feel it's getting too much.'

'I'm OK.'

She bowed her head and went back to work, and Armand stepped away and started snipping alongside her, the pickers on the other side of the wire moving along as they did. For a while nothing existed but the job at hand, though all were aware that the light was fading fast, and that the distant rumbles of thunder were getting ominously closer. They kept their heads down until at long last they reached the end of the row.

'That's it,' Armand said with satisfaction. 'You can give me those snippers now, Caroline. You've done a great job.'

Calli straightened her aching back. 'You mean we've finished?' As she looked up at him her hand flew to her mouth, a gurgle of laughter rising to her throat. She glanced down at herself, and then reached up to feel her hair, and when their eyes met again they both burst out laughing. They were coated from head to foot with a sticky mud of red dirt and grape juice, and there were leaves in their hair, making their heads resemble the trimmings of a bird's nest.

An explosion of thunder overhead wiped the laughter from Armand's lips. He turned and yelled along the row of vines, 'That's it, everyone! Load up those trailers so we can get them in! We haven't much time!' He turned briefly back to Calli, catching her hand and turning it over, palm upward. The soft skin of the first finger had a broken blister and a reddened area round it.

'More suited for writing copy or playing a gentle instrument, mm?' he murmured teasingly, his eyes burning into hers for a second, making her breath catch in her throat. 'I want you to go back and and have a long, soaking hot bath. Agnes will bring a dinner tray up to your room—and some salve to put on your hands. Have your tea in bed and then turn out your light and have a good night's sleep. You won't have any trouble sleeping—take my word for it! Now off you go—run! That hailstorm's likely to hit any second!'

'Armand, I——'

'*Run!*'

She ran.

CHAPTER TEN

CALLI woke up to find a breakfast tray beside her bed. She hadn't even heard anyone come in. She hauled herself up on to one elbow, groaning as she moved, feeling stiff and sore from her labours of the afternoon before. There were fresh croissants and hot bread rolls on the tray, and a jug of freshly squeezed orange juice.

And a single rose in a slender glass vase. A *red* rose. As she reached out to touch a velvety-soft petal with her forefinger she noticed a note propped up against the vase. Her heart jumped as she read the signature. It was from Armand. *He*, not Agnes, must have picked the rose!

She gulped back a surge of emotion as she read,

No need to get up yet. You're not missing anything! Stay there all morning if you want to. I'll be in the winery inspecting the grapes and seeing to various things. Hope you're not feeling too sore. You're a real trouper! Is there anything you won't turn a hand to? See you at lunch.

It was signed simply, 'Armand'. Well, what did she expect—'love'?

'Well!' Armand's face lit up as he turned and saw her just as she was lowering her camera, having caught him examining a handful of grapes from yesterday's picking. The hailstorms had long since passed, and the sky, though still overcast, was brightening by the minute. 'How can you look so good after your first-ever foray

156

into grape-picking? You look wonderful. But you should have rested until lunchtime.'

And missed the few valuable hours remaining to her in his company? Calli smiled, and shook her head. 'I've had enough rest. I feel great.'

She swallowed as he stepped over and gently took her right hand in his, frowning as he bent his head to examine it.

'Fine, huh?'

'OK, I'm still a bit sore, but I enjoyed every minute. Just yell out any time you need a pair of hands.'

'I might just take you up on that.' Meaningless words—her week here was almost over—but they warmed her none the less.

'Were the grapes all right?' she asked anxiously. 'You got them all in in time?'

'Every one. Come and see.'

The rest of the morning passed all too quickly—the winery was buzzing with action, now that the grapes were all in—and Calli made sure she didn't get in Armand's way as he moved around, trailing behind him with her camera. But if she lagged too far behind, or dropped momentarily out of sight, Armand would notice at once and swing round to look for her, calling to her to come and look at this, to cast her eye over that, as if he wanted to keep her close to his side, as if——

Don't think that way, Calli—just don't!

They had lunch in the tearoom off the main office with Lauren and the other office staff—a snack lunch of bread rolls and coffee—and as the others, Lauren included, drifted back to work Armand drew Calli aside.

'Come with me . . . I have something to show you.'

He sounded mysterious, and gently seductive, and when she turned and looked up at him the impact of his eyes almost brought her heart to a stop. The tenderness she saw in the glimmering green depths...what did it mean?

He was standing only a breath away, and she thought for a stifling second that he was going to sweep her into his arms, right there in the tearoom. Her breath tugged at her throat and her mouth opened, forming a soundless 'O' as she gazed expectantly up at him, knowing she wouldn't be capable of resisting him if he did...wouldn't even want to offer any resistance. Dimly she thought, This is how poor Stephanie must have felt...paralysed with love for him.

Even the thought of Stephanie could no longer affect the way she felt about him.

In actual fact, Armand did no more than brush the side of her cheek with his fingertip, but that was enough to light a flame inside her and send it licking downward through her trembling body.

She asked, with a tremor in her voice, 'Wh-what is it you want to show me?'

'You'll see.' He pulled her arm through his and led her downstairs, through the lobby off the kitchen to the narrow door leading down into his private cellar. As he unlocked the door and switched on the lights Calli felt her heart skip a beat, remembering the last time she had come down here, alone. Armand had not been so tender then! She still remembered the cold glitter in his eyes, the way his hands had slid round her throat, the strange, baffling things he had said to her. She had barely had time to think about them since, but now they all came rushing back.

'You want to fetch some more wine?' she ventured huskily as they descended the steep staircase.

'Nope.'

'Then—then why are you bringing me down here?'

'It's time to clear the air. And make up to you for the way I carried on the last time we were down here.'

She bit her lip. What did he mean? Was he intending to present her with one of his rare vintage wines to take home with her?

As they passed along the narrow corridor of bottles he steered her ahead of him, his hands on her shoulders. He didn't speak again until they reached the locked door in the alcove at the end of the row. The room where Hamish had been working the other night.

His hand dropped away as he reached into his pocket for the key, and thrust it into the lock. She held her breath as he pulled open the door and switched on the light inside.

'Go in,' he invited, and wonderingly, still hardly breathing, she stepped inside.

It was only a small room—another cellar of sorts, with wine racks lining the walls, and a table at one end. Her eyes flicked over the green bottles lying in the wine racks.

'These are...a special vintage?' she asked finally, and turned to see Armand smiling down at her.

'Not exactly,' he said. He reached for one of the bottles, and held it out to her. 'With these bottles we're more interested in *this*,' he tapped the cork with his finger, 'than the contents of the bottle.'

'You're more interested in the *cork*?' She stared at him in confusion. 'Why? Are you having some trouble with them?'

He laughed. 'You've no idea what I'm talking about— have you?' he said, shaking his head. 'Come here.' He led her to the table, on which stood a metal apparatus, surrounded by scattered corks. 'Do you know what this is?' he asked.

She shook her head.

'It's a mould injector, used for fitting corks into bottles.'

'Oh.'

He picked up one of the corks. 'This isn't real cork, if you look closely. It's a fine imitation... Hamish's brainchild. A synthetic cork,' he spelt out. 'We're hoping it will be even more effective than the real thing. It's as flexible as cork, only it won't shrink or deteriorate over time. Hamish is still testing it. Testing and refining. He's been working on it for some time. It's the testing part that takes the time, of course. Testing its qualities in the bottle, over a period of time.'

'I see.' Calli was beginning to see daylight. The secrecy. Armand's concern about security. Why Hamish was always working after hours. 'And meantime you feel you have to guard it, keep it a secret...' She looked up at him. 'You don't honestly think someone would try to steal Hamish's idea?'

'We don't just think it, we *know*,' Armand said grimly. 'Other wineries have got wind of what Hamish is doing—it's hard to keep a thing like this a secret. We've had to keep the Wine Research Board informed, and, no matter how careful you are, people talk. One winery we know of would give anything to get hold of the formula and refine and develop it themselves—and earn the credit for it. So we've had to be careful, take precautions.'

'Even from me?' Calli asked, suddenly becoming still. 'That's why you were angry when you found me down here alone... wasn't it, Armand?' Her eyes had widened in mingled hurt and anger. 'You thought I'd come down here to steal Hamish's formula! Or make off with a few sample corks, maybe!'

'No, Caroline!' Armand caught her arm, wincing at the stark pallor of her skin and the pained expression in her eyes. 'That is, I wasn't sure . . . not then. You see, this other winery would go to any lengths. They could have approached you before you came here . . . seen your job here as good cover, and offered you—well, anything, to do a little snooping for them.'

The blood drained from Calli's face. 'I don't believe this!' she whispered. How could he have believed such a thing of her? How could he? 'You thought that I——' She broke off in disbelief.

A twinge of pain flitted across Armand's features. 'Now that I know you, I could horsewhip myself for even contemplating it.'

'Then *why*——?'

He shook his head. 'It was just that . . . well, it was finding you in my office the other night, for one thing. For all I knew, you could have been looking for a copy of the formula. And finding you in Hamish's laboratory that time. Until he assured me you had only come to get material for your article, not to sneak off with anything. And making your phone calls from town, not from here. And then, on top of all that, finding you down here alone in the cellar, outside this very room . . .'

'Oh, Armand, I can explain all that!' The time had come to tell Armand the truth—to tell him who she was, admit she was Stephanie Fox's sister. If he reacted badly and sent her away—her heart twisted at the thought— at least she would have her story, and still have her job. It wouldn't be what she wanted—but then, that would have been reaching for the moon anyway. She had always known that.

'You already have explained,' he said, drawing her with infinite gentleness into his arms. 'You had a perfectly good reason each time for being where you were . . . *I* am the one to blame, the one who needs to make amends.'

'No, Armand——'

His mouth came down on hers, stifling the rest, and only when he felt her grow still did he draw back far enough to murmur against her lips, 'I'm afraid I've been a bit paranoid lately. There's already been one other attempt, you see . . . But that doesn't condone——'

She stopped the rest with a kiss of her own. No wonder he had been feeling a bit paranoid! That other winery had a lot to answer for! 'Oh, Armand, I don't blame you for wondering about me.' The irony of it all hadn't escaped her. Because of her own secrecy, her own mistrust of *him*, she had given him good cause to wonder about her . . .

She looked up at him, her eyes misty, wondering. 'Armand . . . why did you decide to show me this now?'

He met her gaze, his eyes telling her things she would have given the earth to believe, but didn't dare.

'I wanted you to know that I trust you, Caroline.'

She drew in a deep, ragged breath, asking huskily, 'What makes you so sure you *can* trust me?'

He chuckled softly. 'If you had really been here to spy on us, or steal from us, you've had ample opportunity in the past couple of days. While we were fighting that fire nobody would have noticed if you had slipped away. And yesterday, with the grape-picking, you didn't have to offer to help. You could have pleaded your assignment, taken a couple of photographs, and then disappeared—nobody would have missed you.'

'Wouldn't you, Armand?' she asked, gently teasing. And wondered how she could tease at a moment like this, with her own secrets, her own lies and deception, still lying between them. She couldn't let it go on . . . she had to tell him. 'Armand——'

'Hush.' He pressed a finger to her lips. 'Aren't you going to let me answer your question?' He pulled her against him, holding her tenderly, almost reverently against him, so that she could hear the erratic thudding of his heart. 'You honestly think I wouldn't have missed you?' he murmured. 'You haven't noticed that I look for you every moment of the day, that I want you close beside me every moment of the day?'

His fingers had somehow got entangled in her hair, and his other hand was doing tantalising things to her spine through the soft wool of her sweater. His touch was sending hot shivers along the nape of her neck, rendering her incapable of coherent thought, his nearness the only thing at that moment that mattered.

'Caroline . . . you feel the same . . . don't you?'

Ripples of pleasure ran through her as she felt his tongue sliding along her lower lip, skimming over her teeth, then flicking inside to taste the sweetness of her mouth. She momentarily imprisoned the marauding tongue with her lips, drawing a low groan from his throat. As she released him he raised his head and stared at her mouth, his eyes like a shimmering green sea under the harsh fluorescent light. He was breathing audibly, and she heard her own breathing quicken in response.

'Caroline . . . my lovely Caroline,' he said hoarsely, taking her face into his hands, his gaze devouring her flushed cheeks and languorous eyes. Dropping his hands to her shoulders, he crushed her to him again, his mouth claiming hers with renewed urgency, a hungry wildness in the pressure.

She gasped for air as his mouth left hers, letting out a sigh as he buried his lips in the smooth hollow of her throat. From there he rained a stream of tiny kisses downward, inflaming her senses with each teasing touch of his lips.

With warm, urgent fingers he peeled aside the front of her blouse and sank his lips in the creamy swell of her breast. As the heat of his breath seared her skin she made a sound deep in her throat that drew an answering groan from Armand.

'Caroline...' He raised his head and looked hard into her face. 'You do forgive me for ever doubting you, don't you?' The repressed anguish in his voice tore at her heart. 'I should have known you would never be involved in anything underhand...'

She shuddered involuntarily. She might not have tried to steal Château Broch's secrets, but she was being underhand in another way, and when she confessed to Armand how could he be other than hurt and disappointed in her? He might even turn his back on her, despising her for her hypocrisy and deceit. And how could she bear it if he did?

'Oh, Armand, I'd forgive you anything,' she whispered, knowing it was true, and wondering whether he would be able to do the same.

'Caroline... beautiful Caroline! I didn't think women like you existed any more.' His voice, soft and low, sent a thrill flittering through her. 'You make me *feel* things I never thought existed any more.'

She looked up into his face, and his eyes caught hers, hanging there in a moment of naked revelation, his inner emotions glaringly revealed for the first time.

Shock waves exploded through Calli, half-wonder, half-disbelief, and she couldn't hold back a smile—a dazzling smile that burst from within. Was it possible that she had correctly read the look in his eyes, that what she saw there was something deeper than friendship, deeper than lust—a love to match her own?

Dared she think about such things, with the doubts and deceptions that still lay between them and the secrets they both still had from each other? She knew she mustn't, and with a muffled cry she pulled back.

'Darling, what's wrong?'

A tremor ran through her. 'Darling', he'd called her. She gazed up at him, steeling herself for what she had to tell him. It wasn't going to be easy. She didn't want to see the tenderness fade from his eyes, his face harden and grow cold, a wall grow between them. And how would she feel herself when he finally unburdened himself about his treatment of her sister?

'Armand, please let me go.' She couldn't think properly with him standing so close.

He merely smiled. 'I know...it's hardly the place for a romantic tryst, is it? The harsh light...the cold floor... Let's go back, shall we, and find somewhere more...comfortable?'

'Armand, it's not that——' It would be so easy to give in, to lose herself in his arms, and leave any talk until later. But she mustn't! 'There's something I have to tell you.'

'Mm?' He didn't sound worried. 'Damn it, you look so kissable!' He gathered her into his arms again, and treacherously she felt her resolve weakening.

'No!' she whispered. 'Please, Armand...'

'It's all right, my darling. I understand. I *know*. You still don't altogether trust *me*, do you?' He drew back his head. 'Look, I know I haven't been exactly a saint in the past. But I've never met a woman before who's made me care enough to want to give up the life I've been leading. But with you, Caroline, it's different. *I'm* different. I couldn't imagine my life without you.'

Her eyes misted over as they met his, and saw the tenderness there. He will understand, she thought, a warm glow flowing through her. He'll understand why I had to deceive him.

He was standing so close that she could feel the heat from his body, his warm breath fanning her cheeks. 'You think it's all happening too quickly—don't you?' he asked gently. 'But time has nothing to do with it. I know how I feel. And I know I'm not going to change. I want you, Caroline. I never want to let you go! And you feel the same. *Don't* you?'

She bit her lip. 'Yes...no! I mean—Armand, please let me go! When you're holding me like this I can't think!'

His grip slackened, but he didn't let her go. 'Look me in the eye and tell me you don't feel the same way I do.'

'Armand, it—it's nothing to do with feelings. There's something we have to talk about first.'

'Ah. You mean precautions.'

'No! I'm not talking about——' She broke off helplessly. 'Armand, we can't! We mustn't...not until we——'

'Not until we get married?'

'Wh-what?'

'Until we get married. You *are* going to marry me?'

Two spots of vivid colour leapt to her cheeks. The spectre of Stephanie, so dim and distant these days, rose suddenly between them, her sister's lovely dark eyes pained, her red lips twisted in reproach. She seemed to be saying, 'You're stealing the man I love—the man I still want to marry—and might have had a chance if only you weren't in my way!' In a rush of despair, and shame, Calli sagged in his arms, mumbling, 'Do you propose to every woman you want to make love to?'

She felt him stiffen, and draw back. 'You would still rather believe your fellow gossip columnists than take my word.' It was a bleak statement, not a question.

Her eyes widened in dismay. 'Armand, it wasn't——'

A shout from somewhere deep in the cellar reached them, echoing along the silent rows of bottles.

'Armand! Are you down there?'

'It's Agnes.' Armand's hands slid from her arms, leaving her feeling strangely bereft. He shouted through the open door of the little room, 'Coming, Agnes!' He gave Calli a brief, frustrated look, then bundled her back to the stairs, where Agnes met them. 'What's up, Agnes?'

Agnes looked from one to the other, the curiosity in her small dark eyes quickly masked. 'There's a gentleman to see you, Armand. A Mr Tony Day. Lauren says he rang from town a couple of hours ago to see if you'd be home this afternoon.'

Armand grunted. 'Never heard of him. Did he say what it's about?'

'No, he didn't. He says it's personal.'

Armand's brow shot up. He glanced at Calli, an ironic smile on his lips. 'Can't be an irate husband. I've always steered clear of married women.' He shrugged. 'Guess I'll have to see him. Come too, if you like,' he said indifferently. He was speaking to Caroline Barr Smith, journalist, now, she realised. 'I've no secrets from you,' he added in a softer tone. Not any more, he seemed to be saying. But there's still Stephanie, a tiny voice niggled at Calli. Her sister was still there between them. And my deception, Calli thought heavily, is still there too.

Tony Day was waiting in the elegant entrance hall, standing just inside the front door. He was tall and blond-haired, with the physique of a prize fighter. As he shook hands with Armand he said, 'Good of you to see me, Mr Broch,' and added mysteriously, 'Would you mind stepping outside for a moment? There's someone who would like to speak to you.'

Armand frowned. 'Why outside? What's this all about?'

Tony's answer was to swing open the front door and stand aside to let Armand pass through. Calli followed behind, nervously fingering the camera hanging from her shoulder. She had the strangest feeling about all this. She wasn't sure why.

She saw Armand halt abruptly in front of her, halfway down the steps, heard him rasp a question. 'What the hell are you doing back here?'

Calli's gaze flickered past him to the figure standing at the foot of the steps. She almost tripped. A cry escaped her lips before she could stop it.

'Stephanie!'

CHAPTER ELEVEN

CALLI'S sister was wearing a flowing purple and gold top over loose gold trousers, and she looked breathtaking. Calli's shocked gaze took in her sister's familiar mass of dark curls, her flawless skin tanned to a smooth golden brown from the Queensland sun, her lovely face vibrant with health and apparent happiness, with not a trace of her recent suffering in the lustrous black eyes.

Where, Calli wondered dazedly, was the pathetic, heartbroken creature she had last seen?

Armand swung round. 'You *know* her?'

There was disbelief in his eyes. And something else, something remote and unreadable that brought the memory of her sister's anguish suddenly, vividly into Calli's consciousness. She forced her legs to move, to propel her down the steps. 'She's my sister,' she said, tilting her chin. Why had Stephanie come back? And why *now*, just as she was about to confess everything? Her heart twisted inside her. Her sister had come back because she was still in love with Armand. And she still wanted him. Why else? But would Armand want *her*? Either way, what hope was there for Calli Smith? How could she bear to find happiness at her sister's expense—even if Armand was to forgive her for deceiving him?

As Stephanie noticed Calli for the first time her dark eyes widened, then narrowed, hiding whatever she was feeling inside. 'Calli! Why are *you* here?'

'Why are you calling her Kelly?' Armand rapped out.

'Calli, not Kelly. Everyone calls her Calli.' Stephanie cast a puzzled look from one to the other.

'Not everyone.' Armand's tone was ice-cold.

'Calli, why did you come?' Stephanie's lovely eyes clouded. 'I told you to stay away! Don't tell me you came here to look for——'

Armand's voice lashed out, flaying Calli like a whip. 'She's here because blood is obviously thicker than water. Like sister, like sister,' he sneered. He jerked his head round, the force of his icy green gaze compelling Calli's eyes to meet his. 'Lord, what a fool I've been! You actually had me believing in you—believing that you were different!'

'Different from what?' Calli flung back, stung by the sarcasm in his tone, the coldness in his eyes. Where was the tenderness she had seen only moments ago?

'Different from other women. Different from your sister!'

Calli leapt down the steps to slip a protective arm round her sister's shoulder. 'Haven't you hurt my sister enough? You can leave her out of this!'

'How can I...? You're both tarred with the same brush. Both equally capable of deceiving the people you pretend to care for.' The chill in his voice numbed Calli's veins to ice. 'You don't know what honesty and loyalty are all about! Either of you!'

'Now hold on——' Tony Day, hovering behind, took a step forward, but a look from Armand halted him in his tracks.

'This is between Caroline and me—or Calli or whatever she calls herself,' Armand rasped. His look impaled Calli. 'You should have been an actress, like your sister. You've certainly put on a polished enough performance since you've been under my roof. I had no idea that you had taken up where your sister left off. You fooled everybody. You sure had *me* thoroughly fooled.'

As Calli reeled under his attack Stephanie, surprisingly, came flying to her defence. 'There's no need to hit out at my sister because you're still sore at *me*, Armand Broch. I guess I deserve your contempt—but she doesn't. She knows nothing about any of it!'

A harsh laugh from Armand showed his disbelief. 'You expect me to believe that? Oh, no. Too many things add up now. Mind you, she was very convincing. Those eyes...that face...she could talk her way out of anything! And coming here under cover of that assignment was a master stroke. Hell, I should have known she was too good to be true! You're a pair of clever, conniving little bitches. And your innocent-faced little sister is even cleverer than you. Because, unlike you, she almost got away with it. If you hadn't turned up she just might have!'

Calli's head was spinning. This was a nightmare! None of it made any sense. Armand was carrying on as if they had both done something terrible! What did he mean— 'almost got away with it'? Almost got away with *what*?

'Can't you see my sister doesn't know what you're talking about?' Now Stephanie's arm was around her sister, she was the one who was doing the comforting. 'Calli is as straight and as genuine as they come, Armand Broch. Her only crime, as far as I can see, was not telling you she was my sister. And that's——'

Armand's voice grated over hers. 'No, because she knew she'd never win me over if I suspected she had anything to do with you. What puzzles me is why *you* came back. Were you afraid I might not be so forgiving next time—if your precious sister was found out?'

'I didn't even know Calli was here!'

'You honestly expect me to believe that?'

'Yes, I do, because it's the truth!' Stephanie tossed her mane of dark curls. 'And, for what it's worth, Armand Broch, I came back here to apologise! You were good enough to keep your word and not say anything about...what happened. I wanted to thank you for that. And to tell you I regret what I did. It was a damn fool thing to do—I'd never do anything like it again, no matter how desperate I was.'

She turned to face her sister. 'So...it was your newspaper that sent you here. Now I'm beginning to see daylight. You just came here to do a job. And you didn't tell Armand you were my sister because of that story I spun you. Oh, Calli, what have I done to you?'

'Story?' Calli echoed dazedly. She was avoiding looking at Armand; couldn't bear to meet those cold, disillusioned eyes. 'You mean—none of it was true?'

'It seems you're both master story-tellers,' Armand put in scathingly. 'I'll leave you both to sort it out between you. I've heard enough stories to last me a lifetime!' He swung on his heel, mounted the steps in a couple of strides, pushing past a discomfited Tony Day on his way, and vanished through the open doorway, slamming the door behind him.

Calli was left with the bitter echo of his final taunts. She felt as if a part of her had died. Her heart was in tatters, her head reeling in a nightmarish kind of fog. She didn't understand any of it. All she knew was that Armand didn't trust her any more—would never trust her again. The coldness, the mistrust in his eyes had made her heart shrivel up with agony. What made it even harder to bear was seeing the pain behind the coldness in his eyes. She had hurt him badly—irrevocably. But there was more behind his hurt than the simple fact that she had deceived him about who she was. And her sister knew what it was all about!

She became dimly aware that Stephanie was waving Tony Day away, that at the same time her sister's dark eyes were burning into her face, watching her changing expressions. 'He's fallen for you, hasn't he? And you've fallen for him. Oh, boy, if that isn't one of life's little ironies! Armand Broch, of all men!'

When Calli didn't answer Stephanie examined her face more closely. 'It's true, isn't it? You *have* fallen for him, and, knowing you, that'll mean hook, line and sinker. Damn the man! He'd better not hurt you! And he could, you know. From what I've seen and heard of Armand Broch, he's not the marrying kind. And you—my poor pet—are.'

'You told me he'd asked *you* to marry him,' Calli accused bleakly.

'Oh, lord, I did, didn't I?' Stephanie's mouth twisted. 'And so you thought that he—— Oh, my dear, what have I done to you? Look, I said a lot of things that night that I never should have said. I was in such a state— well, you saw me, darling. I was traumatised—petrified that Armand was going to break his word and tell the Press what I had done!'

Calli drew in a deep, tremulous breath. She had been afraid to ask, but now she forced out the question. 'Just what did you do, Steph?'

'You mean he honestly didn't tell you? No, of course he didn't. He's a man of his word. And you, because you had a job to do here, kept quiet about what *I'd* told you . . . about what you *believed* had happened. And yet you still fell for him, regardless!' She shook her head wonderingly. 'Oh, Calli, dear, you'll have to know now. I was hoping you'd never find out!'

'Tell me, Stephanie,' Calli said quietly, a thread of iron in her voice hiding the utter desolation she was feeling inside.

'OK, I will. But please, Calli, dearest, don't you turn against me too. I couldn't bear that. That's why I didn't tell you in the first place.'

'Stephanie . . . tell me,' Calli said warningly. Only the faint trembling of her lower lip betrayed her tension.

'OK, OK, I'll tell you. I was a damn fool, that's what I was. When I came here to shoot that film I was terribly in debt, you see. Well, you know me—extravagant as they come, and hopeless with money. When this guy from another winery approached me and offered me a simply dazzling amount just to get my hands on some silly little half-developed formula, or a few synthetic corks, so that his lab people could work on the idea themselves—develop it a different way, perhaps, a better way—I mean, what was so wrong with that? Oh, yes, yes, I know it *was* wrong, but the way he put it to me——'

'You mean you did it for the money,' Calli said bluntly. 'Under cover of your film, you agreed to spy on Armand in his own home. To *steal* from him. Oh, Stephanie, I don't believe this!'

'Well, you'd better believe it, because it's true.' Her sister's beautiful face hardened. 'I haven't had the easy life you have, darling. I left home when I was still virtually a child, and I've fought my way up to where I am now without any help from anyone! I haven't always been proud of the things I've done along the way, but I've never deliberately hurt anybody—at least not anybody less well off than myself. Armand's got every-

thing—what could a little thing like a new closure for a
bottle matter to him? Whereas, to me, it meant a lot—
security, being able to pay off my debts, new
clothes——'

'It was wrong, Steph, and you know it.'

'Yes, well, don't think I haven't suffered for it! For
one thing, I was only paid a pittance—in advance. And
then Armand caught me in the act. Lifting just a handful
of his precious sample corks! He threatened to call in
the police—and, worse, the media—if I didn't leave the
château right there and then. What could I do? I was
petrified he'd break his word...that everyone would find
out...that I'd never get work again! I couldn't tell you
the truth, Calli—you least of all! That's why I made up
that story about Armand asking me to marry him, why
I told you he'd ditched me for Roxy Manning.'

'You mean *none* of it was true?' Calli stared at her.
'You and Armand never——?'

'Oh, Armand and I did have a mild fling together—
though he took some persuading.' Stephanie's lip curled
ruefully. 'And he made it unnecessarily clear that that
was all it was ever going to be—a bit of fun, with no
strings attached. But everything I said *about* him, Calli,
was true. He *is* the most attractive man I've ever met—
though Tony's not bad either. But no, it wasn't true about
him leaving me for that—well, she used to be a slut; I
see she's actually engaged now. I only threw that bit in
to make it all sound more credible, and to get your sym-
pathy so that you wouldn't delve too deeply into what
really happened.'

'Oh, Steph, how could you? Surely you could have
confided in me—your own sister?' Those piteous tears
of Stephanie's, which had torn her heart to shreds, hadn't
been tears of anguish, but of self-pity and frustration!

'I couldn't tell anyone—you least of all!' Stephanie's eyes pleaded with her. 'I couldn't bear the thought of you, Calli—the person I love best—knowing I could do a rotten thing like that. I couldn't bear the thought of *you* turning against me, despising me. You're my haven, Calli—the one person in all the world that I can turn to, rely on—the one person who never criticises or judges me. Now I suppose you do hate me. Especially for spoiling what you seem to have found with Armand.'

Calli shook her head sadly. 'I don't hate you, Steph—how could I? You're my sister and I'll always love you. I'm just disappointed that you felt you couldn't be open with me. It would have saved me an awful lot of heartache—on your behalf as well as my own. I never would have come here in the first place.'

'And you never would have met Armand,' Stephanie said sympathetically. 'You poor darling! I hope you haven't fallen too hard, little sister. You're not as resilient as I am.'

'Don't worry.' Calli couldn't hide the bitterness that rose to her throat. 'He won't want anything to do with me after this. He's convinced we're two of a kind. And I did come here under false pretences, hiding the fact that I know you. He loathes that sort of thing...deceit...lies...people snooping around...and I did snoop around. Would you believe I almost read his diary once? And he caught me in his cellar another time, when I went down to look for your diamond. I found it too. You'll be pleased about that.'

'You did? Oh, darling!' Stephanie gave her a hug. 'Bless your heart for worrying about your foolish sister, and for going to the lengths you did.' She asked curiously, 'Calli, dear, why *didn't* you tell him about me? Why didn't you face him, accuse him?'

Calli shrugged. 'I guess because I was on a job. I thought he'd send me away if I did. And I...I hated him so much when I first came here that I even had thoughts of exposing him, if I could find a way. But in time I came to know the real Armand Broch, and I...'

Stephanie finished for her. 'You realised he wasn't the monster I'd made him out to be.'

'No. I was going to tell him everything—now, today— but you arrived before I could. And now he knows——' Calli gulped back a sob. 'And I didn't even get to tell him myself! He'll n-never trust me again!'

Stephanie patted her arm. 'Darling, give him a chance to cool down and think things over. If he cares for you at all—and it wouldn't surprise me if you're just the type of woman who would demolish a man like Armand Broch—then he'll see there's nothing to forgive—he'll realise you were totally in the dark about that damn-fool caper of mine. You never know, he *might* even marry you. Stranger things have happened. And you needn't worry that you'll have your wicked sister around to put a blot on your happiness. Tony's putting me on a plane to Hollywood tomorrow.'

'To Hollywood!' Diverted, Calli stared at her.

'Yes, I've had a few nibbles, so I'm flying over to have some talks. Tony's hoping to follow later.'

Calli glanced round to where Tony Day was leaning against a shining sports car, watching them out of the corner of his eye. She asked, 'Who is Tony, exactly?'

'He used to be Australia's top surfing champion—until he was snapped up to star in a mini-series.' Stephanie eyed him fondly. 'He's quite a hunk, isn't he? Good actor, too. We met in Queensland—he was having a few days off too. We've been going together ever since. Nothing serious, of course. We've both got our careers to think of. Darling, I'll be coming back, of course, for the première of *The Winemaker*. You never know, I might even see *you* there—with Armand.'

Calli shook her head. 'There's no hope of that. It's over.'

'Not if I can help it! Look—everything will be all right, darling, I promise you. I'll make it right—it's the least I can do for my little sister. I'll go and find him now.'

'He won't listen,' Calli said dully.

'Oh, yes, he will. I got you into this mess, Calli, and it's up to me to get you out of it.'

'You don't know Armand as well as I do. To him, a relationship has to be based on trust. And he won't trust me again, no matter what you say to him. He'll be disappointed—disillusioned—that I chose to believe you and not him. He told me all along that I could trust him, but I—I never quite could.'

'Of course you couldn't—because I'd made him out to be such a heel!' Stephanie smiled unworriedly, trying to coax a smile in return. 'Darling, you have nothing to reproach yourself for—and he'll see that. I'll make him see it.'

Calli caught her sister's arm. 'Steph, maybe I should come with you.'

'You're afraid he might throttle me when he hears the lies I told you? Oh, Calli!' Stephanie gave her a wondering look. 'Even now you're thinking of me rather than yourself. Don't worry, darling, he'll be only too pleased to hear the wicked story I spun you, and to know that I'm even more of a bitch than he thought me.'

'But what if he threatens to tell the Press, Steph?' She recalled that that was her sister's main fear the first time.

Her sister looked surprisingly unworried. 'Don't think I'm being entirely selfless, love. He's not likely to expose me if he's keen on my sister, is he?'

Calli bit her lip. 'That was before...'

'Darling, think positive! Look, honey, you go and freshen yourself up. Wait for him... I'm quite sure he'll come to you.' She kissed Calli's cheek. 'I'll say goodbye now, pet. After I've seen Armand Tony and I will have to fly. I'll ring from the airport tomorrow, and you can tell me how things turned out.'

'Better ring my flat in Melbourne,' Calli said despondently. 'It'll be a miracle if I'm still here. Steph, you take care... and I wish you all the best. You'll keep in touch, won't you?' As she gave her sister a final hug she wondered if her good wishes were for her sister's career—or if she was thinking more of Stephanie's imminent confrontation with Armand.

'Sure. Bye, darling—and chin up. I believe in miracles!'

'Bye, Steph.' As Stephanie darted across to tell Tony what she was doing Calli turned towards the door, pausing to wave to Tony Day on her way inside. As she mounted the winding staircase to her room tears pricked at her eyes. The way Armand had looked when he'd marched off earlier, there was little hope of his even agreeing to see Stephanie, let alone listening to what she had to say. There had been so many lies and evasions already... why *should* he listen?

She pulled out her suitcase and flung it on to the bed, blinking away her tears, trying not to give in to the misery that was threatening to engulf her. Within minutes she had packed all her clothes, and only a few toiletries remained to be thrown in at the last moment.

Stephanie had tried to buoy her up with talk of miracles. Calli heaved a sigh. Might as well wish for a dream to come true as for a miracle to happen! That was her whole trouble—she had been living in a dream-world, and it was high time she woke up. It was over. She had let Armand down. No matter what Stephanie said to him, that was how he would see it. As a betrayal of trust.

If only she had never come here in the first place! Then she would never have met and fallen in love with Armand. She wouldn't be suffering this torment now. And neither would he.

Was he suffering? She gave a bitter, fractious laugh. Armand had appeared more angry than tormented, more affronted than bitterly hurt. He saw her as another Stephanie. Conniving deceivers, the two of them. 'Like sister, like sister.'

His reaction had hurt her. He hadn't even listened to Stephanie's defence of her—he hadn't even tried to understand. He had simply turned and walked away. He'd heard enough stories to last him a lifetime, he'd hurled back at them.

No, he would never listen to what Stephanie had to say. He would think she was making up this story too. He would never believe either of them again. And, in a way, she couldn't blame him.

How would Leila and Hamish take all this? she wondered, biting her lip. She couldn't bear the thought of hurting Armand's sister. She had been so kind to her— almost like another sister! I'll see her before I go, Calli decided. I'll tell her I never meant to hurt *her*. I'll tell her my side of the story—and leave her to make up her own mind about me.

Although the afternoon was far from warm, she found the atmosphere in her room stifling. She knew she would go mad if she stayed up here, watching the door, waiting to see if Armand was going to come to her. What if he didn't? What if he was expecting her to simply pack her things and go? Her week here was almost up anyway, and she had quite enough material and photographs by now to prepare a superb feature article.

But what she needed right now was some fresh air. A chance to clear her head before the tasting-room closed for the day and she sought out Leila.

She slipped down the back stairs and left by the side-door, breathing deeply as she ran through the rose-scented garden, glad of the sharp, cool breeze on her flushed face. She glimpsed one or two cars in the vis-itors' car park and knew that the tasting-room hadn't yet closed for the day. There was no sign of Tony Day's sports car in the drive. Had they left already? A cold hand closed over her heart. Surely that wasn't a good sign?

It could mean that Armand had refused to see Stephanie. Or it could mean... Calli's hand fluttered to her throat. It could mean that her sister had got cold feet at the last moment and had changed her mind about going to see him.

The gold-tipped vines, stripped of their burden of ripe grapes, looked deserted and cheerless without the brightly coloured pickers moving between the rows. As she headed along the first row the vines on either side rustled in the breeze. It was as if they were whispering a sad farewell.

Her footsteps led her to the lagoon, the water a smooth grey sheet under the overcast sky. The whole world ap-peared grey this afternoon... as grey as her mood.

She found her thoughts drifting back to the balmy evening when she had impulsively stripped off her clothes and lowered her naked body into the cool water of the lagoon. She recalled the moment of shock when Armand had found her there, her face flaming even now at the memory of the liberties he had taken moments later— liberties he had thought she was inviting deliberately. Worse, liberties she had done nothing to repel, because his touch had transfixed her in some electrifying way that no other man's touch ever had.

'What are you planning to do?' asked a deep voice from behind her. 'Go skinny-dipping again? Or are you thinking of drowning yourself?'

She froze where she stood, her mind spinning back to the present, wondering if she was dreaming. *Armand's* voice! How different it sounded now, she thought in bemused wonderment. Where was the coldness and the anger now?

Without turning round, she managed to answer in a tone to match his, 'Well, it's too cold to go skinny-dipping... and if I intended to drown myself I think I would prefer to drown in a vat of wine.'

'We try to keep foreign bodies out of our wines.' He was close behind her now, his voice sending strange vibrations through her, vibrations she knew she must control or she would lose control of her mind and her heart as well.

'I don't feel like a... a foreign body,' she admitted wistfully, a forlorn do-or-die sensation giving her the courage to speak the truth. 'I've come to love this place— the winery, the valley, the... people.' She gulped, emotion choking her throat. Resolutely she turned to face him, glad of the fading afternoon light which blurred his features and dimmed the power of those startling green eyes.

She cleared her throat. 'Armand, I'd like a chance to say goodbye personally to—to Leila and Hamish, before I leave.'

In the dimness something flickered in the shadowy depths of his eyes. 'I went to your room before I came looking for you here,' he said coolly, as if she hadn't spoken. 'You've packed already, I see.'

'I've packed—yes.' She tilted her chin. 'But I don't intend to leave without saying goodbye to... everyone. Please, Armand—that's all I ask. I won't tell any *stories*, if that's what you're afraid of.' A thread of bitterness laced her words.

'You haven't enjoyed hiding things from me, have you?' he asked quietly. 'Coming here without telling me that Stephanie Fox was your sister. Having to hide the fact that you believed I was some kind of monster.' So Stephanie *had* told him! 'As a journalist, what a chance you had to expose me... living under my roof for a whole week!' His tone was impassive, his expression equally unreadable. But, underneath, how bitter and angry he must be feeling! 'How you must have hated me when you first came here.'

Her eyes fluttered away. 'I didn't know you then. But yes—I did, at first,' she admitted, remorse throbbing through her voice. 'And I admit I did have thoughts of... revenge when I first came here.' She kept her eyes lowered, unable in her shame to meet his eye. 'I never should have taken on the assignment. It was wrong, but I—I couldn't get out of it.' She gave a helpless sigh. As if he was going to believe that! She squeezed her hands together, wondering why she was bothering to defend herself. He would never forgive her!

Forcing herself to look up at him, she said passionately, 'Armand, I hated deceiving everyone—especially

you, once I came to know you and . . . like you. I wanted
to tell you, but I—I knew you would send me away if I
did and I—I didn't want to leave! And there was my
newspaper to think of too. If you'd sent me away it would
have meant telling my boss about Stephanie.'

'You mean *they* don't know either that she is your
sister?' He frowned slightly, a frown that tore at her
heart. Now he knew she had been deceiving other people
too! He would never understand—never forgive her.
Never!

She shook her head. 'Stephanie likes the limelight—
I don't,' she explained simply, and shrugged. What was
the use of explaining any further?

'You were going to tell me this afternoon, weren't
you?' he asked softly. 'You were trying to tell me when
your sister arrived.'

She nodded, flinging out her hands in simple despair.
'Armand, I feel so ashamed! I was so terribly confused.
I didn't know what to believe any more. I believed what
Stephanie had told me, and yet—and yet when I came
to know you——'

'Yes?' He was going to make her say it!

'I could see that you were a good man—a man of
integrity. And, besides that, I—you—there was——'

'There was this undeniable chemistry between us?' he
assisted gravely.

'Yes! Oh, Armand, it was awful! I was drawn to you,
and yet—I mistrusted you at the same time! As I came
to know you better I wanted to trust you, but—but
Stephanie was always there between us!'

'And I was drawn to you—but there were times when
I mistrusted you too,' he admitted ruefully.

She gulped. 'I know. I don't blame you. But, Armand,
I can explain all that——'

'You don't need to—I know. Your sister,' he said grimly, 'has a lot to answer for. But at least she has made amends now. I could wring her neck for what she's done to you—to us! Telling you I'd asked her to marry me! No wonder you couldn't trust me!' His brow lowered. 'I always knew there was something there between us. Never once did I think it was your sister.'

'Armand——' she bit her lip '—you weren't too hard on her, were you?'

'For your sake—no, I wasn't.'

'Don't think too badly of her, Armand,' she pleaded. 'She had no idea that I would ever meet you. If I'd told her about my assignment here she would have told me the truth then, and I—I never would have come!'

'Then thank goodness you didn't tell her.'

She reached out to touch his arm. 'She hasn't had an easy life, Armand. She left home when she was very young and she tried living with her father, but that didn't work out either, so she ended up battling on alone.'

'You're a loyal, loving sister. She doesn't deserve you.'

Calli shook her head, her eyes misting. 'I'm all she has. She's never been close to our mother. Or her father. Armand, do you think you can forgive her? And . . . me? Can you ever trust me again?' she whispered, gazing up at him, her eyes straining in the dimness to read his face. 'The lies, the evasions, the underhand things I've done...'

'Now that I know what was behind them I can only wonder that you came to care for me at all.'

'Because I came to know you, Armand. And even before that—well, you only had to touch me and I——' She broke off, flushing.

'Caroline—Calli—whatever name you prefer to use . . . come here!' He pulled her into his arms. 'When you look at me like that I'm a goner...I'm putty in your hands!'

She heard the tenderness, mingled with wry humour, in his voice and a flood of disbelief flowed through her, leaving her as light-headed as if she had been drinking champagne all afternoon. She swayed—and only the fact that she was folded in his arms saved her from falling.

'Who's putty in whose hands?' she asked faintly. 'And you may call me whatever you like,' she invited, her voice muffled as he cradled her head against his chest, murmuring endearments she had never heard from him before, his closeness, the rumble of his voice, the familiar musky tang rising from his body intoxicating her more surely than the most powerful Château Broch wine. 'As long as you call me something,' she added softly, 'and I am around to hear it.'

'Oh, you'll be around all right, my dearest, I promise. I'll need someone to take care of me when Leila and Hamish leave me in the lurch. In fact, I might need more than just a wife...it's a big place.'

Her eyes widened. He still wanted to marry her? 'What do you mean—*more* than just a wife? You're planning a harem?' she demanded, failing miserably to sound affronted.

'Not a harem exactly. I was thinking more along the lines of a dynasty...' He stroked her silky hair with gentle fingers, his touch kindling a spark inside her that only he knew how to set alight. 'Lord, if you knew how much I love you—need you!' He buried his lips in the soft mass of her hair.

'Oh, Armand...' There was no need any longer to hold the words back. 'I love you too.'

'You know——' he looked down at her in a way that told her all she would ever need to know, without another word being uttered '—I do believe I'm actually relieved to find out that you're less than perfect after all. A saint might have been rather hard to live up to. Give me a flesh and blood woman every time... and you *are* flesh and blood, I take it? You're not going to tell me you've been deceiving me there as well, that you're just a dream, a figment of my imagination?' His voice was teasing, unstrained—and filled with a husky tenderness.

'Flesh and blood?' she echoed, looking up at him, her love shining from her eyes. 'There's only one way to find out,' she challenged boldly. His lips were brushing hers now, making speech difficult. 'Don't you find it a little cool out here?' she asked breathlessly, stirring in his arms. 'Shall we go back inside?'

'Let's go to your room and... unpack,' he suggested hungrily, and without waiting for her answer he swept her off her feet and carried her in his powerful arms past the silent, silvery lagoon, through the tranquil vineyard to the château, leaving the vines nodding and whispering in the wind.

Above them, as they reached the imposing balustrade steps of the château, the dark clouds parted and the setting sun burst through.

Accept 4 Free Romances and 2 Free gifts

• F R O M   R E A D E R   S E R V I C E •

An irresistible invitation from Mills & Boon Reader Service. Please accept our offer of 4 free Romances, a CUDDLY TEDDY and a special MYSTERY GIFT... Then, if you choose, go on to enjoy 6 captivating Romances every month for just £1.60 each, postage and packing free. Plus our FREE newsletter with author news, competitions and much more.

Send the coupon below to:
Reader Service, FREEPOST, PO Box 236, Croydon, Surrey CR9 9EL.

✂ - - - - - - - - - ` N O   S T A M P   R E Q U I R E D ` - - - - - -

Yes! Please rush me my 4 Free Romances and 2 Free Gifts! Please also reserve me a Reader Service Subscription. If I decide to subscribe, I can look forward to receiving 6 new Romances every month for just £9.60, postage and packing is free. If I choose not to subscribe I shall write to you within 10 days - I can keep the books and gifts whatever I decide. I can cancel or suspend my subscription at any time. I am over 18 years of age.

Name Mrs/Miss/Ms/Mr _____ EP17R

Address _____

_____

Postcode _____ Signature _____

Next Month's Romances

Each month you can choose from a world of variety in romance with Mills & Boon. Below are the new titles to look out for next month, why not ask either Mills & Boon Reader Service or your Newsagent to reserve you a copy of the titles you want to buy — just tick the titles you would like to order and either post to Reader Service or take it to any Newsagent and ask them to order your books.

Please save me the following titles:		Please tick	✓
DARK RANSOM	Sara Craven		
TAKEN BY STORM	Sandra Field		
LESSON TO LEARN	Penny Jordan		
WALK UPON THE WIND	Patricia Wilson		
WHIRLPOOL	Madeleine Ker		
COERCION TO LOVE	Michelle Reid		
LOVE RULES	Ann Charlton		
HIDDEN MEMORIES	Vanessa Grant		
MAID FOR MARRIAGE	Sue Peters *(Faraway Places)*		
THE SINGING TREE	Anne Weale		
LOVE IS A RISK	Jennifer Taylor		
MIRACLES CAN HAPPEN	Stephanie Howard *(Starsign)*		
BLOSSOMING LOVE	Deborah Davis		
STRONG MAGIC	Christine Greig		
THE STORY PRINCESS	Rebecca Winters		
GOBLIN COURT	Sophie Weston		

If you would like to order these books from Mills & Boon Reader Service please send £1.70 per title to: Mills & Boon Reader Service, P.O. Box 236, Croydon, Surrey, CR9 3RU and quote your Subscriber No:..(If applicable) and complete the name and address details below. Alternatively, these books are available from many local Newsagents including W.H.Smith, J.Menzies, Martins and other paperback stockists from 8th June 1992.

Name:..

Address:...

....Post Code:........................

To Retailer: If you would like to stock M&B books please contact your regular book/magazine wholesaler for details.

You may be mailed with offers from other reputable companies as a result of this application.
If you would rather not take advantage of these opportunities please tick box ☐